AN Angel in
the Middle
by
Nicola Hedges

AN Angel in the Middle

by
Nicola Hedges

Cover art and illustrations by Rebecca Beesley.

Published by Blue Poppy Publishing.

ISBN: 978-1-911438-45-8

For my lovely friends
Sandra and Rosie
With lots of love

By the same author.
Cici: A Dog's Tale - 2020
ISBN: 978-1-911438-13-7

Chapter 1

"My, my, Alex, you are in a hurry this morning, aren't you?" Jimmy called out as the taunting began.

Tommy joined in with exaggerated helpfulness. "Let us escort you to your new classroom."

Harvey quickly took up his position, walking really close behind Alex, boxing him in.

Alex felt the panic rising. He was scared, but he stopped suddenly, hoping that they would carry on down the corridor and leave him behind, but they stuck to him like glue.

Harvey deliberately walked straight into the back of him, heaving him forward with his chest. He accidentally caught his foot on the loose heels of Alex's shoes which threw him off balance.

"Oops! Pick up your feet!" Harvey said loudly, grinning.

Having found a new trick to torment Alex, he stamped on the back of one of Alex's shoes and stood fast. With his foot suddenly pinned down, Alex lurched forward, fell, and landed hard on his knees. His shoe came off and lay like a small, bedraggled animal with its mouth open in a lopsided scream.

The boys laughed loudly as Alex picked himself up without making a sound and slipped the shoe back on. He felt humiliated, and his knees really hurt. He hobbled forward a few steps, but then the pushing began.

"Which way is it? This way?" Jimmy shoved him.

"That way?" Tommy shoved him back.

Alex felt like a small, frail craft on a stormy sea as they shoved him from side to side in the corridor. He wanted to scream at the three boys, but he knew from past experience that it was better to be silent. All he could do was to move as fast as he could to the door of his classroom. They would have to walk further on for theirs.

"See you later!" Jimmy shouted out as they parted ways. Anyone listening would think he was his friend rather than his tormentor. None of the children streaming along seemed to notice Alex's distress.

He dived into his new classroom and scuttled, with his head down, to an empty desk at the back. The teacher had not arrived yet, and the children were busy catching up after the holidays. The sound of their excited chatter reverberated in the big room. Thankfully, no one paid any attention to him.

He felt shaken and tearful after his ordeal. The combination of his heightened emotions, the noise in the room, and the anxious anticipation of the new teacher were overwhelming.

Alex sat rubbing his knees and trying to control his erratic breathing. He blinked away the threat of tears. He realised despairingly, that things had not changed.

Harvey was his older brother, and yet seemed to hate him. At home, he would either ignore or tease him. He and Scott, his younger brother, were always together and excluded him. At school, Harvey actively encouraged his friends to pick on him too. Alex could not fathom out what he had done to deserve this negative attention. They seemed to have taken up where they left off last year, but with renewed vigour.

A few minutes later, the class went quiet as the teacher entered.

"Good morning, everyone! Just in case anyone has ended up in the wrong place, I am Mr Dear, your new class teacher. I will see you at the beginning of each session and some of you for maths lessons as well. Aren't you lucky? Okay, as we seem to be all present and correct, I will quickly do the register."

As he called out each name on the list, Alex studied his face. He was relieved to find that he looked gentle, kind and relaxed.

"Fantastic, we have a full house! Let's all do our best to keep it that way for the rest of the term.

Okay?" He sounded very optimistic, despite a few negative grumbles from some of the children in the class.

"Assembly will be a bit later than usual today which gives me a chance to get to know you all a bit better. I would like each of you to tell me your name and then something about what you have been up to over the summer holiday.

I will start. My name is Mr Dear." The children groaned. "Some of you already know that my passion is sailing. No, unfortunately for you, I wasn't shipwrecked on a desert island." The children laughed and booed.

"I sailed around the Greek Islands and went swimming in some caves. It was truly amazing. The water was such a vibrant blue colour where it was deep and then azure where it was more shallow. It was so clear, you could see right to the bottom and some areas of the sea floor were covered with orange and purple corals. Some caves were hung with the most extraordinary stalactites. In one place, we were able to swim with dolphins. I was sad that we did not see any loggerhead turtles. Next time I go, I hope to see a very ancient, underwater city. Okay, that's me done. Let's start with you at the front and we'll work our way along the rows."

Alex remembered this format from last year. He listened as most of the children talked about their caravan or camping holiday. Some had visited relatives or been to the seaside. Quite a few had been hop picking in Kent. Debbie moaned that she had a horrible holiday because she fell off her bike on the evening of the last day of term and broke her leg. She had to have it in plaster for weeks and weeks. She got a vote of sympathy.

Mr Dear appeared interested in all the contributions, asking questions and making funny comments.

As each child had their say, Alex found himself getting agitated, but also excited. He knew it would be his turn soon, and he was itching to tell the class about his holiday. He was the last child to speak and it all came out in a rush.

"I stayed with my gran. Her garden backs on to an enormous field with a shallow stream running through a bit of it, under the trees. There's a brilliant tyre swing there. Me and Patrick, he lives next door to my gran, went really high on the swing and sometimes we jumped off into the water. We got soaked. We raced each other round the field to dry off. My dog, Willow did everything with us – well, she couldn't go on the swing, obviously!"

Alex drew breath and continued. "After we had our dinner, Freddie, he's Patrick's big brother, let us sit on his motorbike and wear his helmet. We pretended we were Eddie Kidd doing daredevil stunts. Patrick has this big tattoo of a fierce, roaring lion on his arm. I'm going to get one like that when I'm older."

Mr Dear raised his hand as if to draw the tale to a close, but Alex was on a roll and carried on.

"My gran makes the best bread pudding and we had loads of broken biscuits out of the big tin in her kitchen."

There was just so much that he wanted to share, and it felt so good to be transported to a happy, carefree time.

"My gran gave me my first plant, but she looks after it for me at her house. It's a 'sensitive plant' and the leaves sort of close up and it goes to sleep when you touch it, like magic. You mustn't touch it too much or it'll die."

As Alex drew another deep breath, Mr Dear quickly thanked him. The bell went and it was time for assembly.

While Alex was talking about his holiday, he had found himself smiling. He had a lot of good times and adventures in that field with Patrick. They were the same age, but because Patrick lived quite a few miles away, they had to go to different schools. Alex felt his life would be so much better if they were in the same class, better still, if he went to Patrick's school.

Mr Dear had gone to the door and the children lined up in twos behind him. Alex was right at the end of the line on his own which was his preferred position.

He hated being in the hall with all the lower school. At best, he could sit on the end of a row, but he still felt crowded by the mass of bodies and sounds.

When everyone was settled, Alex focussed on the staff seated on the stage. He listened attentively to what was being said, enabling him to block out any distracting noises nearby.

Mr Adams, the headmaster, enthusiastically welcomed everyone back to school.

"I have very high expectations of each and every one of you. The start of the new school year signals a fresh start and a time to set goals. Some of you did really well in the end of year exams so you need to think about reaching for excellence through continued hard work and diligence. Some of you have just been simmering. You need to stoke the fires of learning and bring yourselves to the boil, as it were, so that you can reach your full potential. Those of you who have been struggling and lagging behind, for whatever the reasons, need to take charge and really apply yourselves. What happens to you in school will have a great impact on what happens to you when you leave. You need to take advantage of all the help you are offered and make yourselves proud of improved grades and achievements knowing that you have done your best. Let us all make this the best year possible in work, sport and other activities."

There were notices from some of the other teachers before each class filed out of the hall and down the corridor to go to their lessons, one long line after another. The sound of all those feet tramping and thudding with squeaking and tapping shoes, reverberated unpleasantly in Alex's ears.

The morning lessons passed quickly and, before Alex knew it, the bell went for lunch. He had to walk past the entrance of the dining hall on the way to his locker. There was a snakelike queue of children inside waiting to collect their school dinner. The din was horrendous; clattering plates, scraping chairs, jangling cutlery, overlaid with loud chatter and laughter. He felt so thankful that he had been able to opt for packed lunches every day and so did not have to sit in that hall. It meant that he could eat his lunch somewhere quieter, or outside if the weather was fine.

He collected his lunch from his locker. It was his favourite - a cheese and pickle sandwich on white bread and a strawberry flavoured drink. Alex always prepared his own packed lunches the way he liked them, and he chose the same thing every day.

He was feeling happier now. Despite his run in with his brother and friends, it had been a good morning. He liked his class teacher, he loved remembering and telling all about his holiday times at his gran's and he enjoyed the English lesson.

He liked Mrs Knight as she was very good at breaking down the instructions so that he had no difficulty in understanding what was expected. She had a deep voice which carried well to the back of the class. Alex loved reading, especially non-fiction and he enjoyed writing. He did not care much for reading poetry though, because he found it difficult to find the hidden meaning in a lot of the poems. Luckily, poetry was not on the agenda for now.

Alex was really enthusiastic about learning. He thought that the more things he could learn, the better. He always held his hand high in the air to answer questions. He was not showing off. He only wanted to share what he knew with others because he thought it was interesting. He did try to stop himself sometimes, as he had learnt that the other children became irritated when they thought he was being a 'know it all'.

Chapter 2

Alex skirted around the busy playground to the grassy bank on the far side. The few, small oak trees which grew there were bending away from the school as if they too wished for peace and quiet. This was his safe place, his retreat. He leant against his favourite tree's rough trunk. Often, he would read or do some writing under this tree.

He thought about his first morning back at school as he munched on his sandwich. Things had gotten off to a really bad start. It actually began last night.

At about nine thirty yesterday evening, Alex and Scott had been sent up to bed by their mum with their uniforms to be put out in readiness for the following morning.

Scott always tried to get ahead of Alex so that he could get into the bathroom first. He seemed to think that his needs were much more important than anyone else's.

As Alex had waited with Willow, his dog, he had looked dismally at his uniform. He hated the fashion of the seventies, with the long, pointy collars and bell - bottomed trousers. It irritated him having all that fabric flapping about.

He had folded the legs of the voluminous, black, flared trousers in half lengthwise, making them look very slim lined. He so wished that he could wear the drainpipe trousers, like the ones his dad had worn when he was younger.

He had picked at the edges of the faded knee patches, indifferently hand stitched where Harvey had worn them through several times.

The (not so) white shirt had looked quite grubby and was frayed in places. He knew that his mum did her best, but shuddered when he thought of the vests, pants and socks boiling away in the big saucepan in an attempt to try to whiten them. He wished his mum would use some of that blue stuff his gran used in her rinse. Clothes seemed to come out much whiter for her.

Then he had folded back the cuffs of the sleeves on the mustardy, yellow jumper. They were always way too long because Harvey had stretched them out so much when he tied them round his waist or played tug-of-war with his friends. When Alex wore them, the end of the sleeves would overhang his fingertips. They kept his fingers warm in the winter though, he thought ruefully.

He had traced the resistant grease marks on the front with his finger. It made him upset that he had to wear this when he loved to have everything neat and tidy. It made him feel very self-conscious.

All their clothes were sent swishing around in the top loading washing machine, were fished out with a pair of wooden laundry tongs and fed through a set of rollers on the back of the machine. They were then rinsed by hand in the kitchen sink and put through the rollers again. Finally, they were hung, all bunched up on the old wooden clothes horse next to the boiler until they were dry.

As he had hung each item on the hanger, he had been able to see that the whole ensemble had been badly ironed. His mum never had time to sprinkle clothes if they were too dry for ironing. Although items were superficially smooth, the fine creases, like cracks in china glaze, were still visible. Alex thought that perhaps he would learn how to iron himself. He had watched his gran loads of times, perhaps she could teach him.

Needless to say his socks, grey rather than white, were odd and one of them had very little elastic. He had rummaged in his drawer for an elastic band to hold it up. He hated the feel of odd length socks and the way they bunched up around his ankles if they fell down.

When he had reached down and picked up his shoes, he had felt a mixture of despair, anger and frustration. They were very worn and scuffed on the toes. No amount of polishing and buffing would make them shine. The backs of the heels were crumpled down because Harvey could never be bothered to untie the laces. When he tried them on, it was like wearing a pair of slippers and his feet slipped out of them. They should have come with a warning.

He shuddered as he knew how uncomfortable he would feel with these clothes against his skin in the morning, especially as they had been Harvey's, and he could be so horrible.

He never complained as he knew that uniforms were expensive and he did not want to upset his mum. Secretly though, he wished that just for once, he could be the one to have a pristine, new school uniform to mark the start of a brand-new school year.

Alex had jumped as the bathroom door had banged open. Scott had thumped along the landing into the room he shared with Harvey. Alex had left his room, carefully closing the door behind him.

In the bathroom, Scott had left his clothes and damp towel strewn all over the floor. He did that every evening. Alex was not sure whether this was because he was lazy or whether he did it just to upset him because he knew that Alex liked things to be tidy.

So many times in the past, he had asked Scott to hang his towel on the hook on the back of the door, to put his dirty clothes in the washing basket and his uniform over the banister or in his room, but he never took any notice. Instead, Scott would say anything he could think of to wind Alex up further.

Resignedly, Alex had hung the towel on the hook behind the door. He had put both their everyday clothes over the side of the bath before having his wash and brushing his teeth at the basin. The flannel had not been rinsed out and the water was almost cold. Ugh!

Back out on the landing, he had stuffed both lots of dirty clothes into the basket. He had noticed with dread that his bedroom door was now open. His heart had sunk as he found all the drawers pulled out and the door of his wardrobe hanging open. He had peered inside them and saw that things had been disturbed. Yet again, his private space had been invaded. He had been left feeling very distressed because things had been moved, and he hated things being in disarray.

Alex knew Scott was responsible as he had a habit of rummaging around and helping himself to whatever he wanted without asking. Alex had tried to explain to him that these actions really upset him, but Scott had just laughed and mimicked someone being really fussy. After that, Alex never tried to explain again. He just reorganised his things and waited for the missing items to reappear at some point, but that did not happen often.

It had been too late last night for Alex to sort his things the way he liked as this involved taking everything out, shaking it; folding and placing it back in just the right place. He knew that he had to be patient and fight off the urge to sort and tidy, and to deal with the mess when he got home from school the next day.

He longed for a lock to be put on his bedroom door to give him some privacy, but his parents told him that 'it was not necessary' and that he was 'overreacting'. They did not seem to understand how important it was for him to be able to keep his things as he liked them and to have a bit of space that was just his.

Alex had finally slid under the blankets in a state of great agitation. Willow had been curled up asleep at the bottom of the bed. She had moved up and settled in the space between his back and the wall. Even so, he had felt unsettled, as if he were somewhere strange. The sounds of 'Fawlty Towers' on the television mixed in with the laughter of his parents and Harvey drifting up the stairs had made him feel a bit better, but then he had begun to worry about his first day back at school.

During the night, he had nightmares. One really bad one was where he had a long, elastic strap tied around him and he could never quite get to his classroom before he was dragged back down the corridor.

In reality, he loved being in lessons, but the other times of the day had been tricky and were not helped by his big brother's bullying.

He had really hoped that things would be different for him this year.

Chapter 3

Alex shook away these thoughts and packed away all his lunch things in his satchel. He watched the other children absorbed in their activities on the playground for a while. He thought it was a bit like watching television. There was so much going on. He lost himself in the 'entertainment' for a while, switching channels whenever he felt like it.

It was all happening right there, in front of him. There was sport; children wrestling each other, racing and, of course, football. There was drama; children acting out their stories with wild gesticulations and exaggerated movements, laughter and tears. There was action; two stocky boys engaged in a serious scuffle with members of staff rushing over as children gathered in a crowd around them.

One of the boys was Lee, who was in the same class as Scott. He always seemed to be in trouble for fighting or hurting other children. The crowd dispersed and the children moved away.

Alex thought he had better go to the toilet which was in the brick building at the far end of the playground. He did not like going there, but the children were not allowed into the cloakrooms until after the bell had gone and then there was always a queue. The cloakroom was a horrible place for him to be as it was so noisy and the children so unpredictable.

He went in cautiously, in case there were other children messing about in there. He did not want to be picked on. There was no one there except for Lee whom he had seen getting into trouble on the playground earlier. He was standing at one of the sinks, but was not washing his hands. His head was bowed and he was staring at something in his hands. It was absorbing all his attention. He did not look up as Alex walked in.

Curious to discover what he was looking at, Alex craned his neck as he walked past him heading towards one of the cubicles. He wished he had not. It was awful. There, in Lee's hands, was a helpless daddy longlegs. Alex had noticed several of them stumbling along the walls as he entered the building. Lee was not admiring it or helping it though, he was systematically pulling its legs off, one by one!

Alex felt physically sick. He could not stand any form of cruelty. Despite Lee being bigger than him and having a bad reputation, Alex could not ignore what he was doing. He had to say something.

"Stop it! Please stop it!" he begged. "That's really cruel. You're torturing the poor thing. That's so wrong. How can you do that?"

Lee said nothing. He simply turned his head and stared at Alex threateningly.

Alex felt uneasy as he slipped into an empty cubicle, quietly closed and locked the door. He really hoped Lee would be gone by the time he came out. He stayed in there as long as he could and then opened the door a crack.

His heart sank when he saw that Lee was still there. The broken bits of the lifeless insect were scattered in the sink. Lee was standing with his back to the sink and was focussed on Alex. He felt his heart race as he began to walk past him.

Suddenly, Lee lunged at him and punched him hard on his arm. Through gritted teeth, he said, "Mind your own business in future or you'll be sorry."

The punch really hurt and Alex instinctively held his arm. He was so shocked that he simply nodded submissively and ran out. Just then, the bell rang. Alex was shaking inside. He made it across the playground, looking behind him several times. Much to his relief, Lee did not appear.

'The Terrible Threesome' was waiting just inside the entrance. Alex had to run the gauntlet again, on top of what had just happened. It took all the courage he had not to react or break down. Getting back to the safety of his classroom only took a few minutes, but it felt like a lifetime.

Alex slipped into his place, hoping that no one could see that he was near tears. He closed his eyes and breathed in deeply. His knees still hurt from the morning's fall in the corridor and now there was a throbbing pain in his arm. He was shaken, not only by the bullying, but by the slow and deliberate cruelty he had just witnessed.

The rest of the afternoon passed in a blur and by the end of the day, Alex was exhausted. He did not want to bump into Harvey and his co-conspirators or Lee, so he rushed straight out of the building and ran home, all the way down the hill.

Chapter 4

Alex leant on his front gate to catch his breath. As he straightened up, something caught his attention. He looked at the three terraced houses in front of him. Alex's house was in the middle.

There was something different. The houses on either side of his appeared to have changed drastically. There were no curtains in any of the windows. The glass windows were dirty and some of the panes were broken. The paintwork was peeling and faded and the front gardens were really overgrown.

The houses looked as if they had been abandoned many years ago. Had he just not noticed that his neighbours had gone? He thought back over the summer. How long had they been like this?

Alex had not known his neighbours that well. Mr Andrew was at no. 15 and Mr Cedric at no. 13. They were both pretty elderly and were long retired. They tended to keep themselves to themselves and did not venture outside very much. When they did, they would always chat for a bit over the garden gate.

He remembered that he used to wave to their houses on his way to and from primary school. When his mum had asked him why he did that, he had said it was just in case they happened to be looking out of their windows and could see that he was thinking of them. His mum had called him a 'funny fish'.

Mr Andrew and Mr Cedric had always thrown balls and toys back over the fence. Sometimes they chatted over the back fence with his mum as she pegged out the washing or with his dad when he was working in the garden. That was ages ago. He could not think when he had last seen them. He ran inside to ask his mum.

His beloved dog, Willow was waiting for him in the hallway. She tried to catch his fingers in her mouth, arching her back and wagging her tail as she wove in between his legs. Alex got down on her level and held her tightly for a moment. She wriggled around and licked his face.

At first, he laughed and play wrestled her but then he could feel all the emotions of the day catching up with him. He did not want to burst into tears, so he clambered up from the floor and went into the kitchen.

Alex's mum did shifts at the local shop from Monday to Saturday. With the exception of Saturday, she made sure she was always home in time to get a meal ready for her family at the end of the day. Everything else had to fit in around her hours.

She was sitting quietly at the kitchen table, having a well-earned mug of tea before starting the chores. The old, brown teapot in its knitted cosy sat in the middle of the table. His gran had made this from odds and ends of wool left over from her various projects. It made a bright and cheerful centrepiece with its faded mirror image in the worn Formica. The tea strainer full of tea leaves was resting on a saucer with the bottle of milk beside it. The light glinted off the glass bottle reflecting a distorted shape of the window. The silver foil top was a bit bent and did not cover the top completely. One of her favourite pieces of music was playing on the radio; 'Albatross' by Fleetwood Mac. She was humming along to the slow and gentle tune of the guitar.

She looked up and smiled, but did not get a chance to ask him about his day, as she would usually do, because Alex began to gabble immediately.

"How come they're empty? Some of the windows are broken as well. I never noticed that they were so overgrown. Where did the old men go? Do you suppose they're still inside?"

"What are you rabbiting on about?" asked his bemused mum.

"The neighbours," answered Alex. "Where have they gone? How come I never even saw them leave?"

"Oh, them!" she replied. "Mr Cedric went to live with his daughter down in Kent, in the summer, as he couldn't manage on his own anymore. Someone in the shop told me that Mr Andrew had been very poorly and had gone into a hospice, I think. I heard that he passed away several weeks ago."

"That's so sad! I wish I'd known they were going because then I could've said goodbye." Alex thought it was awful that his neighbours could have just disappeared like that. It was as if they had never existed. It was upsetting to think he had not noticed them for so long.

His mum interrupted his thoughts. "Never mind the neighbours, how was your first day back?"

Alex focussed on the things he had enjoyed doing in his lessons. He did not want to worry her with the other incidents. She would have become upset, threatened to ring the school and caused a stir, taken his brother to task and then Harvey would have denied everything and found a way to get back at him later. It was not worth it. The telephone rang and his mum went to answer it.

Saved by the bell!

Chapter 5

Alex took Willow for her walk up to Greenleah Heights. He was retracing his morning's journey and thinking about his first day back at school.

That morning, when Harvey and Scott had finished their breakfast, they had grabbed their things and rushed off in excitement. By the time Alex had caught up with them, they were already halfway up the long, steep hill which led to their school. Alex had wondered why he had bothered rushing as Harvey and Scott walked side by side ahead of him as usual, making sure he could not walk with them.

They had chatted about football as they went. This was all that they ever seemed to be interested in. Harvey was a Liverpool fan and ardent follower of Kevin Keegan. Like his dad, Scott followed Charlton Athletic. Mike Flanagan was his favourite player at the moment.

Although it was not his favourite subject, Alex did read bits in the paper his dad brought home, and absorbed the information he heard in other people's conversations. His favourite player was Asa Hartford of Manchester City. Somewhere in one of his books, he had a football sticker of him when he used to play for West Bromwich Albion. Alex could have joined in with his brothers' conversation, if only they had let him.

Alex had wondered if perhaps they were embarrassed at how scruffy he looked compared to them. He had felt, and thought, he probably looked like the poor relation. He had walked along behind them with his shoulders drooping, head down and eyes focussed on the ground, feeling very uncomfortable and conspicuous.

He turned and looked back down the hill as he waited for Willow to investigate a lamp post and gateway.

When he had turned his head briefly this morning, he had seen the children surging up the hill behind him. Some of them had seemed eager, while others had looked as if they were being dragged forward against their will. The whole scene had looked to Alex as though they were being drawn towards the school by the force of a giant, invisible magnet.

In his mind's eye, he had been able to see a magnet, one of those shaped like a horse shoe, rigged up on the top of the school building. It had zig-zag rays like the ones you see in a cartoon, coming out of the ends and down the hill. All the children were like little yellow and black insects flying through the air, dragged against their will by the magnetic force. The image made him smile as he remembered.

At the top of the hill on the left, between the last house and the shop Alex's mum worked in, was a narrow alley. Groups of children sometimes played there after school. It was deserted now.

A bit further on, was the telephone box. Sometimes, the boys or his mum used it to phone home if they were going to be late. That was if they had a two pence coin in their pocket along with their handkerchief and the other odds and ends they seemed to accumulate. Sometimes, a coin would rattle out if you banged it, but Alex never did this. It felt like stealing.

On the opposite side of the road, there was a low, green, metal fence enclosing a large, grassy island in front of Greenleah Secondary School, which was where Alex and his brothers attended.

He stopped and looked for a minute. The school building had two wings either side of the main door, one bordering the road. The playground went along the side of the other wing with a number of wooden benches placed around the edges. The playing fields were at the back.

At the far end of the playground on one side, there was a grassy bank with a row of stunted oak trees and a fence at the top. On the other side, there was a small toilet block. He shuddered as he recalled what he had seen there this morning.

Right in front of him there was a huge, green, wrought iron gate, the entrance to the school site.

This morning, as usual, all the children had funnelled through the gate and had spread out on the playground. It had been very busy. There had been games of football and chase, groups shrieking with laughter and pushing each other about, children calling out to friends and shouting over the general hubbub and excitement of the first day back.

Alex had always hated all the noise and chaos. He was out of his comfort zone on the playground. That morning he had also felt as though he was the odd one out; the one that nobody wanted for their friend. Not even his brothers had stuck around like in other families. Harvey had already disappeared and Scott found Charlie and Stanley, two of his friends from the football team to chat with. Alex had been impatiently waiting for the bell to go, and for order and relative quiet to be restored.

He had seen Harvey meet up with his two friends, Jimmy and Tommy. Jimmy was tall and as skinny as a beanpole and had a mop of curly hair and a big nose. Tommy, on the other hand, was short and plump and had straight, limp hair and sausage-like fingers with nails bitten down to the quick. Alex thought of them as 'The Terrible Threesome'.

He felt a knot developing in the pit of his stomach as he remembered how mean they were to him last year. He had hoped that they might have changed. Well, that had turned out to be a false hope and no mistake, he thought grimly.

This morning, the noise and constant ebb and flow had added to the edgy feeling Alex already had through lack of sleep.

For as long as he could remember, he had been very sensitive to loud sounds and the noise of large groups. When he was little, he would cover his ears and rock if he could not run away to a quiet place. He still found it very distressing, but as he grew up, he had learned strategies to help him cope.

He had headed across the playground to the grassy bank on the far side; to his safe place, his retreat. As he had walked, he had tried his best to keep his body upright to appear more confident than he actually felt. He had stopped next to his favourite oak tree and put his hand on the trunk. He had closed his eyes and focused until he could feel the soothing ripple of the pulse of its life force. Alex loved trees.

He had looked up into the tree which would hold on to its brown leaves for a long time and be one of the last to put out new leaves in the spring. It had filled him with awe and appreciation, and he had begun to feel calmer.

He walked on again, still deep in thought as Willow tugged at her lead.

Alex's favourite time of year was spring when the branches were still completely bare, but were beginning to bud. To him, tree trunks and their larger branches looked like arteries and veins, while the smaller twigs looked like a mass of capillaries. Then, he could really feel the surge of life beneath the bark. Now, in the autumn, that force was slowing down, but he could still feel the comforting rhythm.

As there had been some time before the bell was due to go this morning, Alex had pulled out his notebook and pen and leant against the tree and had started to write.

He always found that this was a very useful strategy to help him feel better whenever he was surrounded by a lot of people and noise. The focus of recalling facts and writing them down calmed him, and blotted out all the extraneous sounds as well as the feeling of isolation.

This morning, he had decided that he would try and write down as many names of inventors as he could, what they invented and the date of each invention. He was very good at remembering factual information.

He had been so absorbed in what he was doing, that when the bell finally went, it made him jump. The pitch of the bell always made his ears hurt and he had to resist the urge to cover his ears.

By the time he had put his notebook and pen back into his satchel, buckled it up and had hurried towards the school building, most of the children had already disappeared inside and the last few stragglers were just going in.

Harvey and his friends had been loitering by the door. They had pretended to be waiting for a mate but Alex recognised this ploy and his stomach had knotted up.

He had taken a deep breath and tried to slip past them, hoping to catch up with one of the groups of children hurrying down the corridor. He had not been quick enough though, and Jimmy and Tommy began their pincer movement, one on either side.

He shook himself and broke into a jog to displace these unpleasant memories. He ran on to the path between the old gate posts with Willow trotting along beside him.

Chapter 6

Greenleah Heights was their favourite place for walks as most people preferred the park and recreation ground just off the main road. Also, it was further up from the school and shop and people did not want to struggle that far up the hill. Often they had the whole place to themselves.

It was a vast expanse of grass mainly, with a large mound at the top. It was all enclosed by metal railings. A long time ago, there had been a manor house and gardens there. There was a view over their part of the outskirts of London from there. His house was on the large estate which stretched up and around the hill.

They meandered along the paths and Alex began to relax. He sat on a bench and Willow jumped up beside him, resting a paw on his knee. It was as if she could feel his sense of sadness.

She was a small dog with an earnest expression. They had grown up together and they shared an unbreakable bond. Although Alex felt he could talk to his parents sometimes, he never felt particularly special to anyone in the way that he did to his furry friend. She was his confidant, and he knew that she loved him unconditionally, and never, ever judged him. She was always there for him whenever he wanted to talk, play, or go for a walk. Alex never tired of her company and she always slept on his bed at night.

He leant over and pulled their heads together. She turned and licked his face. This made him laugh. He jumped up and raced her along the path. He felt so much better.

They walked on until they reached the more open part of the grounds and then Alex took off her lead.

Willow ran round and round in decreasing circles at full speed, growling and snapping at the long tufts of grass or sticks left behind by other dogs. She loved it up there. Alex enjoyed being up there too. He loved having the space and being up above all the people, traffic, and noise. He felt free, just him and his dog under a wide sky.

When Willow was tired, she wandered off to sniff at all the new scents and stopped to nibble some of the longer, juicy blades of grass growing between the railings.

He thought about his neighbours who had left so suddenly and how it must be very hard to be old. He wondered what would happen to the houses now and whether he would have new neighbours soon.

Willow trotted over to him and began nudging his hand. It was her way of saying it was time for a game of fetch. Alex loved throwing the tennis ball for her. When she brought the ball back, he always rewarded her with a little treat.

Sometimes, they would run all the way around the Heights, but not today. Alex needed to get back to sort his room out before dinner and he was exhausted.

Chapter 7

Back home, they raced each other up the stairs to his room. Alex had the smallest room in the house. There was just enough space in there for his bed, which was positioned lengthwise under the window so that he could see out into the back garden, a narrow bookshelf crammed full of books that he had been given as presents over the years, a small chest of drawers, a tall, thin wardrobe and a large brown beanbag. The rest of the space in the room was taken up with stacks of storage boxes balanced almost up to the ceiling. Sometimes, he felt as disregarded as all those boxes which had not been touched for years.

Alex began the task of getting his room back to rights after Scott's invasion. He was very thorough in his sorting out and tidying. He shook out and refolded everything. He placed things carefully where he wanted them. He needed everything to be in its rightful place to feel comfortable in his room again.

Willow had found her favourite space to stretch out on the bedroom floor between the bed and the beanbag for a nap.

Once he had finished, Alex plumped up his beanbag and wriggled himself into a comfy position to do some reading before dinner.

He was halfway through a fascinating book about inventions, when the peace and quiet was shattered by the sound of the front door slamming.

Harvey had been out practising with his football team after school. He flaked out in his room listening to music. He had saved up to get a few records to play on the old record player a friend of his dad's had passed on. He had cleaned it up and replaced the needle and it sounded as good as new. He had bought a single by Pink Floyd and a David Bowie LP at the charity shop in the high street.

Scott had been reading one of his comics. He was not in the mood to listen to music. Harvey turned up the volume, so Scott slammed out of the house and went back up the hill again to play kerbs with Charlie and Stanley in the alley opposite the school.

The smell of cooking wafted upstairs. Alex's stomach began to rumble and he could no longer concentrate on his book even though it was really interesting. He ran downstairs to give Willow some food and fresh water before lending a hand to lay the table ready for dinner and putting up the extra leaf of the table to make it big enough.

"I'm back!" shouted his dad as he passed the kitchen and trod wearily upstairs to change out of his work clothes.

He was a scaffolder and worked all the hours he could get, including overtime. At the end of the day, he was often so tired that he would fall asleep after dinner. On the weekends he was not working, he loved getting out into the garden to tend the vegetable plot he had established.

"Go and fetch Scott. He went to play in the alley by the shop," Alex's mum said. "Why they can't find somewhere else to play beats me. They could go up to the Heights."

"There aren't any kerbs there," Alex pointed out as he went down the hallway to the front door.

Harvey and his dad came downstairs together and took their places at the table. They discussed the football matches to be played at the weekend, arguing about who might win and what the score would be.

Scott and Alex were out of breath, having run all the way back.

"Now you wash your hands properly with soap. I dread to think of what you may have picked up in that alley!" their mum demanded.

"It's not that bad," Scott replied. "We always play up the top end."

"I don't care," said his mum. "Now get on with it as I'm ready to dish up."

Scott turned on the tap and reached for the soap. He washed his hands thoroughly and rinsed them. Before he turned the tap off, he grinned at Harvey and used his finger to aim a jet of water at Alex, who was not expecting the sudden squirt of cold water and nearly tipped his chair over as he ducked.

"What did you do that for?" their mum yelled. "It's gone all over the side and the floor. Get a cloth and wipe it up quickly. Your dad's waiting for his dinner."

Harvey laughed.

"Pack it in!" said his dad crossly. "It's time to eat!"

Scott and Harvey looked daggers at Alex as if it was his fault.

Once Scott was seated, their mum served lamb stew from the big saucepan. Alex tried really hard not to think of the socks and pants previously boiled in it. There were mashed potatoes, carrots, peas and some greens to go with it.

His mum poured some of the water left over from cooking the greens into a cup for Alex. Ever since his dad had told him that the greens water was full of goodness, he always had some whenever greens were on the menu. Alex enjoyed it best when he added some pepper to it.

He eagerly tucked into his mashed potatoes and thought it tasted pretty good, despite the lumps. He ate all the vegetables first and left the stew to last.

Once their mum had sat down to eat, she began to talk about the neighbours.

"Alex was just saying earlier about the old boys that used to live next door. I heard one had gone to live with his daughter down in Kent and the other one has just passed away. He was in a hospice for a while, wasn't he?"

"Yes he was. One of the fellas at work went to the funeral," added their dad. "Mr Andrew used to work in the packing factory so there was a really big turnout at the wake in the local pub. He seems to have been a popular bloke. It's so sad."

"I wonder who will come to live next door," said Harvey. "Hey, we could get a really famous footballer!"

"Yeah, right," muttered Scott, still in a bad mood from being told off. "Famous footballers are well known to live in Greenleah."

"Okay then, maybe just some kids who like to play football," Harvey capitulated.

"Actually," joined in their mum, "having some younger families would be nice. Liven up the place a bit. Get to know them and have a chat over the fence."

"Never mind chatting," said their dad, "how about some lovely, green fingered, retired chap who will have so much time on his hands once he has sorted out his own garden, that he will offer to come and do mine!"

"Oh yes," re-joined their mum. "He will have a wife who loves baking and always bakes too much because she forgets that the kids are not at home anymore, so she shares some with us!"

Everyone laughed. Their mum was not known for her culinary skills.

Feeling full, their dad, Harvey and Scott went off to watch the television. They all loved 'The Sweeney'.

Alex stayed to help his mum to clear away. He enjoyed doing this and he knew she really appreciated it, especially after a long day.

When they had finished, his mum went to join the rest of the family, while Alex went to collect his satchel so he could do his homework at the kitchen table. As he worked, Willow kept a watchful eye on him.

By the time Alex had finished, he would have seen only the very end of the programme they were watching, so he nipped upstairs to get into the bathroom first for a change.

He examined his legs. There was dried blood and a graze on each of his knees. He looked at his arm in the mirror but he was unable to see any evidence of Lee's punch yet. He cleaned his knees thoroughly with the flannel before putting his pyjamas on.

In his room, Willow was already curled up on top of the blankets at the end of the bed, so he shut the door quietly and got into bed. He curled up too and lay there for a while, thinking about possible new neighbours, but it was not long before he fell into an unusually deep and undisturbed sleep.

Chapter 8

The following morning, Alex woke early. It was lovely just to lie still and let his mind wander. There was never any need for the boys to have alarm clocks because Alex's mum yelled at the top of her voice to wake them up. Her voice was so loud, it made Alex's ears ring. He loved his mum dearly, but he felt it was such an abrupt and undignified way to start the day. If only she could wake him up with a softer, more gentle voice.

However, it did the trick as Alex and his brothers were never late for school. He was glad that she yelled rather than doing what his brothers sometimes did. They would sneak into his room and put a freezing cold, wet flannel on his face and scamper off laughing or they yanked his bedclothes off him unexpectedly.

He thought about his mum's voice. When they were out shopping, she had a habit which made him cringe with embarrassment. She would be busy browsing in an aisle which held no interest for

Alex, hair products, for example. Alex would go off to look at the books or magazines.

Suddenly, he would hear his name being called repeatedly as if over the shop's sound system. He would scoot back in double quick time, only to find her still browsing in the same place. She did not seem to realise that he was not a little child wandering off and getting lost and he always told her where he was going.

He rolled over and cuddled Willow who had crept up the bed when he woke. He closed his eyes again and thought about the wonderful dream he had during the night.

Everything seemed so vivid and real. He was in a vast, undulating space. There was a babbling brook and birds singing in some beautiful oak trees. It was a hot, sunny day.

As he looked around, plants and shrubs of all different shapes and sizes began to grow. It was like watching time lapse photography. Before his very eyes, a fabulous garden began to appear.

It was like all the spring times he had ever known, thrown into one moment. It was familiar to him, as if he had been there before. He felt as if he had a glimpse of what Heaven might be like. Alex had felt at once peaceful and energised.

His train of thought was interrupted by his mum bellowing up the stairs, but he did not mind today. He got up and made his bed quickly and rushed into the bathroom first.

Then he skipped downstairs to the kitchen with his dog in tow and started his routine for the day. He gave Willow her breakfast, measuring it out carefully. He washed out her drinking bowl and then filled it three quarters full with clean water.

His mum always made a big pot of porridge to which everyone helped themselves when they were ready. Alex liked to get in first as he preferred his porridge to be runny. If it was too thick, he could not eat it because the texture was wrong and he would have to thin it down with hot water or milk.

He had his favourite place to sit. This was at the end of the kitchen table where he could see out of the window and not have the door behind him. This routine was occasionally disrupted when Harvey decided to play a few tricks. Sometimes, he would sit in Alex's place or he would hide the dog food or water bowl just to get rise out of him. Today was not one of those days.

His mum had just finished making the porridge. She poured some into a bowl for Alex. Thankfully, it was just the right consistency. Then, she poured a cup of tea and helped herself to a bowl of porridge.

His brothers could be heard thudding about upstairs as they got ready. It was lovely to have his mum to himself.

"Here, Alex," she said, "I meant to tell you yesterday. The funniest thing happened at the shop. You know Mr Herbert and Miss Bertram? Well, they both had orders to be delivered. I packed the boxes myself. That new lad, Matthew, who has just started doing deliveries, got them muddled up, so Mr Herbert ended up with sponge fancies, hairspray and a pair of tights.

He came to the shop in great embarrassment. He demanded to know what we thought a bloke like him wanted with hairspray and a pair of tights. Well, we just couldn't help it, we burst out laughing. The comical picture of Mr Herbert in tights! It was so funny, him with his skinny legs and round beer belly.

Then this other woman in the shop told him that he would have been better off with a can of spray polish! Even Mr Herbert had to laugh then and rubbed his bald head. I haven't laughed so much in ages. All morning, we just kept laughing at the picture he conjured up."

"What about Miss Bertram?" asked Alex "Did she see the funny side too?"

"When they sorted it out, Miss Bertram smiled sweetly and said that she had wondered about the beer and pork scratchings and wasn't quite sure how she would get through all those spuds!"

Alex chuckled with his mum as he knew both the victims of the mix up. They were still laughing when Scott and Harvey came into the kitchen and his mum began the tale again.

Alex thought he would take the opportunity to leave a little earlier than normal and walk to school on his own. He had a spring in his step as he walked along the driveway to the front gate.

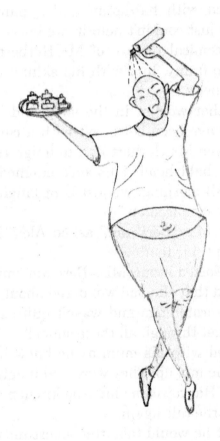

Chapter 9

When he turned to shut the gate behind him, he looked up at the three terraced houses.

What a surprise! There were curtains in all of no. 13's front windows. They were really colourful with a vibrant rose pattern on them and they all matched. The windows looked new and glinted as the morning light shone on them. The front of the house was also now a freshly painted shade of soft pink. It was a lovely, warm colour.

By contrast, no. 15 was like a beacon - the walls, window frames and the blinds at each window were bright white. The sun bounced off the windows. The whole effect was quite dazzling.

He stared, rubbed his eyes and looked again. No, his eyes were not playing tricks on him. He looked back and forth between the two houses, finding it hard to take in the extraordinary changes which seemed to have taken place overnight.

It occurred to Alex that the new neighbours must have moved in already, but then he could not understand how they could have replaced the windows, painted the houses and put up curtains and blinds in such a short time. There had been no sign of anyone around the day before. Surely they could not have done it all in the dark, could they?

It was a lovely, crisp, bright morning. He looked up and saw a beautiful blue sky, in which were suspended the most brilliant white, fluffy clouds. He knew that they were called 'cumulus clouds'.

Alex walked along at a leisurely pace and looked around him as he went, rather than looking down at the pavement as he usually did.

Then he had an odd feeling that he was being watched. The back of his neck felt prickly and there was a strange humming in his ears. He tried hard to resist the urge to turn around but the feeling became more and more intense.

He spun around and looked back, but the only people he could see were two children who were not even looking in his direction as they were deep in conversation with each other. Alex thought that perhaps his mind was playing tricks on him.

He continued walking, but the feeling returned and it seemed to get stronger with each step. Whatever it was, it did not want to be ignored. He whisked around, but he could spot nothing unusual. He felt spooked and was desperate to locate the source of the feeling.

His eyes were drawn to a slight gap at the side of one of the curtains in the upstairs window at no. 13. Was someone there, watching him? Alex stared at the gap for a while. He turned away and then back again really quickly, to try and catch 'them' unawares but he could detect no movement. He could see no one in the windows or gardens of either house. It was weird.

Alex did not know that he was being observed from high above those white, puffy clouds.

Even before he was born, they had been involved in the development of this special soul. They had helped him to begin his life's journey and watched him grow. Now that he was about to become a teenager, they decided the time was right to enlighten him.

Slowly, he turned back up the hill and the feeling of being watched subsided as he switched his attention to thinking about his birthday the following day.

He would be thirteen, a teenager at last. He wondered if he would feel any different. He knew his dad was off this weekend so they would be able to spend time in the garden together.

He also knew that Harvey was spending the weekend at Tommy's and they were going fishing with his older brother.

Scott was playing away with his football team on Saturday and Stanley's dad was giving them a lift. He would probably stay over too.

His mum would be working at the shop. It would be lovely to have the space. She would remember to bring home his favourite cake for him. That was more than enough to make his birthday feel special.

Then on Sunday, he thought he would wash his dad's car. He usually did this and earned fifty pence to put in his piggy bank. His mum and dad had given him this china 'piggy bank' for Christmas when he was ten. It was shaped like a puppy lying on its back with the slot in its tummy. The rubber stopper was underneath on his back. He called it his 'puppy bank'. He liked to save up to buy some nice presents for his family on their birthdays and at Christmas.

Every so often, he felt the weight of his 'puppy bank'. He would shake it gently and try to work out how much money he had managed to accumulate.

He had some old coins in there as well, from before decimalisation. He kept these in a small cloth banker's bag his mum had let him have from the shop. He had threepenny bits, sixpences, shillings, florins, half crowns and a ten shilling note. Some he thought he would keep. His gran had given him several silver sixpences, one on each birthday since he was small and he knew they might be worth a bit to collectors in the future.

He loved the size and shape of the threepenny bits with their pattern of either a portcullis or a thrift plant on one side. He also had several farthings with a beautiful wren embossed on them. They were his favourites. He would keep those, but some of the other coins he would have to change up into the new decimal coins so he could use them.

He kept the 'puppy bank' hidden under his bed, in the far corner, near the wall, at the head of the bed. He covered it with an old bath towel so that his brothers could not see it. He began to think about what he might buy for his mum as hers was the next birthday after his.

Chapter 10

With all his daydreaming, the walk to school had taken him much longer than usual and he was really cold because he had dawdled while he was thinking. He wished he had worn his jacket.

By the time he got to the school gate, he was desperate to use the toilet. He rushed over to the toilet block, thinking that it would be empty as it was still quite early but inside, he was surprised to see Lee at the sink again.

His heart jumped into his mouth as he skidded to a stop. This time, Lee had a beetle in his hands and was about to destroy it, piece by piece. Alex knew that he had to challenge him again so he gathered up all his courage.

"Put the beetle outside on the grass and leave it alone!" he said, in the firmest voice that he could manage. "Why are you being cruel to insects?" he asked. "Is it because you're really fascinated by them?" He was about to say that he could lend him a book if he was interested, but his mouth went dry. He swallowed and licked his lips nervously.

He was amazed when Lee dropped the beetle. It landed in the sink on its back with a tiny, hollow clink. Lee turned towards Alex, smiling. Alex was mesmerised by the slow, rhythmical movement of the beetle's legs as it lay on its back, walking in the air. He noticed that it still had all six legs intact.

Then, as if in slow motion, Alex saw Lee's smile turn into a snarl and watched as his hand bunched up into a fist. By the time he realised what was happening, he was too late to dodge a powerful punch to his stomach. Alex was winded and bent over double, trying to catch his breath.

Lee retrieved the flailing, upturned beetle and disappeared outside with it trapped in the hollow of his hands. Before he left, he gave Alex a parting kick on the shin as he strode past. Alex had done his best, but he knew that there was no hope for that poor beetle now.

He felt sick and was about to wet himself because he had been holding on for so long. He rushed into the nearest cubicle and locked the door. When he had finished, he sat down, clutching his stomach with one hand and rubbing his shin with the other. He drew a couple of shuddering breaths and that was when the tears began to flow.

How could a day which seemed so full of promise, suddenly turn into a mini nightmare?

He was still sitting there when the bell went. He did not want to move. He blew his nose, sniffed and wiped the tears from his red, puffy eyes. Gingerly, he stood up and walked slowly out of the building.

The feeling of relief when he saw that the coast was clear was overwhelming. Alex made his way to the school entrance. He felt drained, but there was a cold spark of anger towards all those who took advantage of defenceless creatures. He was in no mood to tolerate Harvey and his sidekicks who were lying in wait for him.

As usual, they rushed up behind him and took it in turns to push him in the back and to and fro across the corridor. With all the lurching around, his stomach felt worse. He could feel that tears were gathering again. The boys carried on relentlessly. Then suddenly, it was as if the spark had ignited deep in his chest.

He swivelled around. "Leave me alone!" he roared. "I'm not a punch bag for your amusement!" he yelled into their faces. "You're just cowards picking on me all the time because you know that I won't fight back. Well, I won't stand for it anymore!"

Alex's outburst shocked the boys. They stopped in their tracks and stared at him, open mouthed. Everyone turned to look, including a teacher just emerging from a classroom at the end of the corridor.

"What is going on? Why are you shouting in the corridor?" he demanded to know.

Alex was on the verge of speaking up about being bullied when Harvey jumped in as smooth as you like.

"Sorry, Sir," he said. "It's just a misunderstanding, Sir. We are very sorry for the noise, Sir."

Outrage and frustration filled Alex as he stood there shaking and unable to speak. The audacity of it! The teacher did not seem entirely convinced by what Harvey had told him, especially as he could see that Alex had been crying. He had not seen what led up to the shouting himself, so as a now deflated Alex just stood there in silence, there was very little he could do. They all were sent off to their classrooms as they were now late for registration.

By the time Alex arrived in his classroom, Mr Dear had completed the register.

When Alex walked in, Mr Dear stopped talking. All eyes were on him. Just what he needed when he was still feeling so upset! Alex made a beeline for the safety of his desk. He gripped the sides of his chair to stop himself collapsing into a heap.

Mr Dear regained the attention of the class with some announcements which allowed Alex to begin to compose himself. It was time for assembly, so Mr Dear asked the children to line up.

"Go on down to the hall," he told them. "I will be along in a minute." He remained at his desk.

Alex was still in his place, shaking and very pale.

"Would you like to tell me what happened?" Mr Dear asked gently.

Alex longed to tell him the truth, but knew that if anything came of it, he would be made to suffer even more. He could not lie to his teacher so he said, "My brother already explained everything to the teacher in the corridor. I can only apologise for being late."

Mr Dear raised an eyebrow, but accepted what Alex said and chose not to make an issue of it as he could see he was still upset.

"Go and wash your face and get your things from your locker ready for your first lesson," he suggested kindly. "You are in here with me for maths anyway. The others won't be back for a while so take the time to calm down before we start the lesson. I must go down to the hall now."

"Thank you, Sir," Alex said very shakily as he took a couple of deep breaths. Then he did as Mr Dear suggested and returned to his place feeling a little better.

He normally loved maths, but his emotions were still churning so he decided he would not put his hand up in class for the rest of the morning. He did not want any attention whatsoever.

It was a relief when it was time for lunch.

Chapter 11

Outside, Alex shuffled slowly across the playground towards the grassy bank where he sat under his favourite oak tree.

He was not interested in looking at anyone or anything. He closed his eyes and tears began to seep out. He wanted to be anywhere but here and be anyone but Alex. The familiar tastes of his lunch were comforting. The support the tree gave him felt reassuring too.

He made himself think again of the lovely dream he had last night and then suddenly, it was as if he was actually in that beautiful garden. The plants looked as if they had grown a little. It was wonderful to be back there. He felt safe. As he sat, his breathing began to slow and a sense of calm descended on him. He did not want to leave this tranquil paradise. He stayed there for as long as he could before he reluctantly opened his eyes.

He stood up and stretched and was surprised to notice that the pain in his stomach and shin had completely gone.

Although it was still a little too early, he decided to go into the school before it was time. He did not want everyone staring at his blotchy face and red eyes or asking questions, and he certainly did not wish to encounter any of the bullies.

Luck was on Alex's side. The older boys were fooling around on another part of the playground and he managed to sneak inside the door without anyone noticing him. He almost ran down the corridor.

He sat on the floor, hugging his knees just outside his classroom. He kept breathing slowly and tried to find that inner calm and peaceful place again.

When the bell sounded, Alex was the first to enter the classroom.

It was Friday afternoon, and all Alex had to get through now was a double lesson of PE. He collected his kit bag from his locker. He had not examined it beforehand and dreaded the collection of mismatched items he was sure to find.

In the boys' changing room, he tentatively loosened the cord on the bag and his heart sank as he pulled out Harvey's old kit.

He saw an off white tee shirt, two off white socks of different lengths, skimpy black shorts and a pair of black plimsolls which had definitely seen better days. Reluctantly, he put everything on and kept to the back of the group as Mr Roberts, the PE teacher led them out onto the large sports field.

Mr Roberts started the lesson with warm up exercises. Alex enjoyed doing them as he stayed focussed on copying the teacher's every move. A couple of girls close by giggled uncontrollably. Alex hoped they were not laughing at him in his PE kit. He did not have time to dwell on this as the whistle then went for them to run a lap around the outside of the football pitch.

Alex jogged on the spot until everyone had started running to make sure that he would be right at the back and then he set off at a steady pace. He was last to finish, but he felt very pleased with himself. He was not at all puffed out. He knew that if he had been running on his own, his time would have been one of the fastest because he ran so much with his dog. The run had done him good. He could breathe deeply without shuddering and he felt energised.

They were to play a game of rounders next. Alex was really pleased that Mr Roberts had organised the teams beforehand. At least he would not feel awkward waiting to be chosen.

Alex threw himself into the game, fielding well and when it was his turn to bat, he managed to get a couple of rounders for his team. When the final whistle went, he was feeling much better. He had actually enjoyed the game.

With a few children delegated to carry the sports equipment back to the PE cupboard, the class filed back into school. They were all changed and ready just in time for the bell at the end of the day.

Alex walked home alone. It had been an eventful and tiring day.

As he approached his front gate, he stopped to look at the houses on either side of his.

The front lawns in both gardens had been mowed. They looked perfect and now there were long, empty, flowerbeds surrounding all four sides of no. 13's rectangular lawn. There was a single, large, empty circular flowerbed in the centre of no. 15's lawn. Alex thought that whoever his new neighbours were, they must be very keen gardeners.

He gave a cursory look at his own front garden and felt a little ashamed when he saw the overgrown lawn and flowerbeds full of nothing much but some dahlias beginning to go over, a few scrubby bushes and well-established weeds.

He was itching to see who his new neighbours were. His eyes scanned their front gardens and windows in an attempt to see them, but there was no one around. Somehow he felt sure that one or other or both of them had been watching him this morning. It was as if there was some connection between them.

Indoors, Alex was met, as usual, by Willow. She chased around in circles and wagged her tail with excitement. Alex bent down and rewarded her with a gentle cuddle and a stroke under her chin before they both clattered upstairs.

Alex heard his mum call out. She was in the bathroom, finishing off the cleaning in there. He popped his head round the door.

"Hi Mum," he said. "Have you seen anything of the new neighbours yet?"

"No, I haven't. There wasn't anyone outside at the front when I came home," she replied, much to Alex's disappointment. "Didn't see anyone at the back either when I hung out a bit of washing," she added.

Alex went to his room and climbed onto his bed to see if there was anyone out in the back garden now. Willow jumped up too and pressed her wet, black nose against the glass. She was looking out of the window as well, moving her head from side to side.

Although he did not see anyone out there, he did see that both lawns in the back gardens had been mowed. They too looked perfect and there was not a weed in sight. Alex realised that strangely, both back gardens were set out exactly like the front ones.

Thinking about the curtains and blinds he had noticed in the morning, Alex reckoned that if he stood at the end of his own back garden and looked at the back of both houses, they would have identical curtains and blinds to those at the front.

He decided to test his theory so he leapt downstairs and rushed out into the back garden. His dog thought it was a great game. Past the shed, the swing and the makeshift slide on one side, past the greenhouse, through the vegetable patch and past the compost heap to the bench standing against the back fence, they raced.

Willow cheated as she could get under the obstacles which Alex had to go around. Alex plopped down on the bench and surveyed the backs of the houses on either side. Sure enough, he was absolutely right. They were mirror images!

Alex was amazed at how hard his neighbours must have worked to get the outside to look that good so quickly. There was something very pleasing about the neatness and symmetry.

Alex sauntered back to his room. He plumped up his beanbag and wriggled into it until he was comfortable. Willow jumped onto the bed and curled up into a tight ball. Alex felt a bit guilty because he was too tired to take her out for a walk now.

He quickly lost himself in one of his books about flowers until his eyelids felt really heavy and began to close.

Soon Alex was back in the beautiful, heavenly garden. It was so real. The plants looked as if they had grown even taller and now they were almost in bloom.

As he walked leisurely along the garden path with the comforting warmth of the sun on his back, he took in the wonderful fragrances which wafted on the gentle breeze. All his senses were so alive.

He felt that he belonged in this garden. Although he could not see or hear anyone else, he felt that he was not alone.

He turned slowly around to see if he could spot anyone, but there was no one there. He was in a part of the garden that he had not visited before. The plants were different and he bent to have a closer look.

Then he felt the strangest sensation. It was as if he was being pulled away from the garden by an unseen force. The colours blurred as he seemed to fly backwards at speed. He heard a sound. At first, it seemed far away and he could not make out what it was. Then it was closer and, with great clarity, he heard his name being called. His body twitched. He opened his eyes.

Alex felt disorientated and looked around him to get his bearings. He was surprised to find that he was still sitting on the beanbag. His book was lying closed on the carpet in front of him. Willow was still on the bed but was looking at him now with her head on one side.

He heard his name. It was his mum shouting for him to come for his dinner. Although Alex did not feel hungry, he dragged himself up and went downstairs slowly. He felt as if he was sleepwalking.

The rest of the family were at the kitchen table and their plates were nearly empty.

"What's the matter with you, Alex?" his mum wanted to know. "We've all finished and your food has gone cold. Why didn't you come down when I first called you?"

"Sorry Mum," he mumbled. "I fell asleep."

"You're not sickening for anything, are you?"

"No. I'm okay, just tired."

"So soon?" she wondered.

"Not just that…" he said, leaving it hanging and then added, "it's been a long day."

Before anymore could be said, Alex dropped his eyes to his plate and began to eat. Digging into his corned beef, cold potatoes and beans, he listened to the tail end of his brothers' accounts of their day at school. He thought how different their days had been.

While they had enjoyed spending time with their friends at school and playing football after school, he had to endure being bullied and feeling isolated for most of the day. He noticed that Harvey had conveniently left out the part where he and his mates had bullied him. If only his parents knew how unkind he could be.

When it was Alex's turn to tell about his day, he looked directly at Harvey, who suddenly seemed very uncomfortable.

"My day started out really badly," Alex replied honestly. "It did improve though and I did well in my rounders' team."

It was lucky for Harvey that he was not questioned any further, otherwise he might have said something. His dad looked at him as if expecting more, but decided to leave it. The conversation petered out.

Harvey and Scott left to spend some time with their mates for a bit while their dad went into the front room, switched the television on to watch the news, but promptly fell asleep.

Alex's normal routine was out of sync tonight so he rushed the rest of his dinner, gave Willow her food and a change of water. He quickly made his packed lunch, which was his usual cheese and pickle sandwich on white bread, with a strawberry drink he mixed from 'Nesquik' powder and milk. Then he helped his mum to clear everything away. After that, it was time for him to get on with his homework.

He decided to do it while sitting on the beanbag in his room rather than at the kitchen table. He had a page of multiplications to do which he found really easy and it did not take him long to complete. Alex loved numbers. He could remember number sequences easily.

Although it was Friday night, Alex did not want to stay up late and watch television as he was normally allowed to do. He was not that keen on game shows like 'The Price is Right' or the science fiction films that Harvey liked. Instead, he was quite content to get ready for bed and spend the time in his room with his dog curled up beside him.

Alex stroked and tickled her. She loved it. She rolled onto her back and lifted her paws in the air. Her mouth was open, and it looked as if she was grinning. She was in a playful mood. Alex let her gently nibble his fingers as she wriggled and rolled. She was such fun. He wished he felt this happy with his brothers.

It was getting dark, but before settling down, he had another peep out of his window to see if there was any sign of his neighbours. There was no one there. He snuggled up with Willow and dozed off. Almost immediately, he found himself back in the beautiful garden.

Chapter 12

When Alex woke the following morning, he felt really refreshed. His recurring dream seemed to have a marvellous effect on him.

He sprang out from under the blankets, knelt on his bed and pulled the curtains back. He threw the window open and stretched his arms in the air as he greeted the beautiful, sunny day.

He stopped mid-stretch for there, in the back garden of no. 13, was a woman kneeling on the lawn beside an empty flowerbed. Her trousers and top were covered in a bright pattern of large, exotic, multi-coloured flowers.

Alex was mesmerised as she drew a large circle with one of her fingers just above a bare patch of soil. Seconds later, it was filled with pink asters. Alex rubbed his eyes, not quite believing what he had just seen. She drew another large circle. This time, deep pink flag lilies appeared. On she went until all the beds were full of beautiful flowers which were every conceivable shade of pink. It was amazing. The drifts of plants seemed to be woven together in an intricate design. Not a patch of bare earth could to be seen. How did she do it? Was it some kind of magic?

He did not know how long he had been watching her. He was in a bit of a daze so when she turned and deliberately looked up at him and winked, he continued to stare at her with his mouth open. He suddenly came to and felt really awkward, but it was too late to pretend that he was doing anything other than staring. Still looking straight at Alex, she smiled and waved to him. It was as if she knew him. Alex was surprised and a little bit pleased. He managed a slightly nervous smile and waved back to her before he flopped back onto the bed.

Alex was aware of the humming in his head that he had heard the other day.

When he sat up again and looked out, the flowers were still there, but she had gone. His dad was at the end of their garden. He had his head down as he was busy working in the vegetable patch. He was totally unaware of what was going on next door, behind the fence or of the strange encounter. If only he knew!

Today was Alex's birthday and he was now thirteen years old. It was his first day as a teenager. He was so relieved his birthday fell on a Saturday this year and that he did not have to go to school today.

When he glanced at the little clock on top of the bathroom cabinet, he was surprised to see that it was already ten o'clock. It was not like him to sleep in that late. No wonder his dad was well into the weeding already.

Alex leapt down the stairs two at a time. He put the porridge on to reheat, adding water and stirring vigorously to get rid of the lumps. His dad must have made it earlier. There was no sign of his brothers. It was one of his mum's days at the shop. He let Willow out and then fed her.

There were four birthday presents on the kitchen table. He sat in his chair and looked carefully at each one. Two were from his parents and were addressed to him and there was one from each of his brothers which were addressed to Willow. They always shared the same birthday.

He opened the ones from his parents first and was delighted that they had given him two non-fiction books, one about gardening and another about insects.

He served himself a big bowl of porridge, and then he opened the presents for Willow on the floor. Alex slowly peeled the wrapping paper off. She barked and wagged her tail in excitement, sniffing and trying to grab them. There was a new tennis ball and a bag of treats. Alex was really pleased with all the presents. He gave Willow a few treats which she wolfed down and then looked around for more.

Apart from the clicking and scrabbling of Willow's claws on the lino as she chased her new ball, it was blissfully quiet. It was a special day, not just because it was Alex's birthday, but because he and his dad would get to spend quality time together in the garden as no one else was around.

He cleared away quickly and then went out into the sunshine with his faithful friend trotting happily behind him, carrying her new ball.

His dad had already made a good start on weeding around the sweetcorn and beetroots and was just beginning to hoe between the rows of leeks. When he saw Alex, he straightened up.

"Happy birthday, Alex!" he shouted. "How does it feel to be thirteen? I can't believe you're a teenager already."

"Thanks, Dad," he replied with a grin. "Am I supposed to feel different then? I don't reckon you can remember how you felt."

"Cheeky!"

"Thanks for the books, Dad. They're great. I can start using them today to find out more about the things we find in the garden. Then I can add them to my little reference library."

"Glad you like them, Alex. We thought you'd like books more than other stuff." He bent to tickle Willow behind her ears. "And did you like your presents too, you lucky girl?"

Willow seemed to be grinning happily. She had her present between her paws as she lay looking at them with her ears cocked and her head to one side.

Alex picked up the pair of garden gloves his dad had brought out for him and got stuck into weeding between the runner beans.

"There are loads of beans still, Dad. Can we pick some for dinner tomorrow?"

"Yes, I should think so, but you see those really long pods with the big bumps in them?" his dad said, pointing to several near where Alex was weeding. "They need to stay, to make seeds to plant next year. I'll dry them in the greenhouse and then put them in an envelope to keep in the airing cupboard until the spring."

He went over to the stand of sweetcorn and squeezed a couple, then peeled the husk back on one of them. He showed Alex the small kernels at the top.

"These will have to stay a bit longer before they're ready, but those bigger ones with the brown tassels are ready now."

His dad was pleased with what they had managed to produce, considering that he did not have that much time to put into looking after the plot. He was often too tired after work or the weather was awful.

The onions were laid out to dry in the sun. The carrots were not as plentiful as last year and the cabbages had not been covered in time to stop them being damaged by root fly, but there was a good crop of courgettes. Some of them had grown into huge marrows.

As Alex worked, he took time to study the insects buzzing around the flowers and popped back indoors to look them up in his new book. He told his dad some of the interesting facts he had read about them. His dad always took an interest, even though he probably knew a lot about them already.

Willow was stretched out on the lawn, basking happily in the sunshine. She opened one eye every so often to check on Alex and only stirred when the flies became too annoying, then she went to lie down in the shade.

By the time they had managed to weed the whole vegetable patch, it was just after one o'clock in the afternoon. They stood back to admire their work. Alex's dad felt thirsty and wanted to have a break. He asked Alex to go indoors and make them both a nice mug of tea and a sandwich which they could have as they sat on the bench. Whilst they were eating, they could plan where to plant the various seeds and bulbs in the front garden.

Alex went back towards the house and his dad looked for the radish seeds in the greenhouse as they might just get a quick crop before the season ended.

On the way to the back door, Alex heard the humming again and then someone saying his name. He stopped and listened. The voice was coming from no. 13's garden. He was really curious to see this new neighbour close up so he moved over to the fence and peered over.

The woman he had seen before from his bedroom window was walking towards him.

Alex still felt a bit sheepish because she had caught him staring at her in the garden earlier. He smiled nervously and she smiled back at him. She seemed genuinely pleased to see him and she introduced herself.

"Hello," she said. "My name is Poppy Longate. As we are now next door neighbours, you can just call me Poppy."

She reached over the fence to shake his hand. As their hands touched, Alex received something like a mild electric shock and, at the same time, the dreams of the beautiful garden he had been having, flashed through his mind. He pulled his hand back quickly in surprise. That humming sound was still there.

"Err...pleased to meet you," he replied nervously.

He studied her face with her rosy cheeks and hazel eyes framed by soft, shoulder length, fair hair. She seemed to be waiting for him to say something more so he gave her the little speech that he always used to introduce himself.

"I'm the middle one of three Angels. My name is Alexander Noah Angel," he said. "As we're now next door neighbours, you can just call me Alex," he added with a smile.

Poppy laughed and it was as if Alex heard the faint sound of voices singing. He shook his head and began to turn away. Poppy turned away too but called over her shoulder.

"I am really pleased to see you again and I look forward to catching up with you soon."

Alex dived into the kitchen and filled the kettle and put it on the gas hob. As he waited for the water to boil, he thought about what had just happened. It was very odd, but probably it would have seemed just quite ordinary to anyone watching.

Poppy had a kindly face and he was intrigued by what she had said. He wondered what she had meant. Had they met before? When? Where? If so, why could he not remember? What were they going to be 'catching up' on? Why had he heard those strange sounds? Why had his dream come back to him in that moment? Was there a connection between his dream and what he had seen earlier in her garden? It was all very peculiar.

The kitchen door banged, making him jump and his dad came in. The kettle began to whistle.

"Where's that mug of tea then, and what about the sandwich? I'm starving." He sat at the table.

Alex spooned some tealeaves into the teapot, added the boiling water and put the tea cosy on. Leaving it to brew, he quickly got the plates and mugs out of the cupboards and then the bread, margarine, cheese, pickle and milk from the fridge.

As he made their lunch, Alex told his dad that he had finally spoken to their new neighbour at no. 13, who was called Poppy. He described her and said that she seemed really nice.

Lunch in hand; they headed back into the garden. Alex's dad peered over the fence to try and catch a glimpse of Poppy, but she was nowhere to be seen.

Alex wanted to switch off all the thoughts and questions which buzzed in his head like the bees around the flowers.

Chapter 13

As it was his birthday, Alex asked his dad to tell him about when he was born. All he knew was that he arrived a bit early and that he had been a little poorly. Secretly, he had often wondered what could have happened to make him so different from his brothers.

"When you were due to be born," his dad began, "Mum was whisked into hospital early. They had to 'phone the office and the boss sent someone to find me on site and then I had to get the bus to the hospital. I didn't have enough money for a taxi and waiting for one to come would have probably taken even longer.

By the time I got there, you had already arrived. When I went to the ward, I saw the doctor. He told me that you had been born really quickly and seemed to be unresponsive.

They had taken you away to do tests and they found that your heartbeat was so slow and quiet, it could hardly be heard. They couldn't understand it as you were all pink and healthy looking."

His dad sat quietly for a moment as if lost in his thoughts. Then he began again. "You didn't cry or open your eyes. They were mystified and decided to return you to your mum and monitor you closely. One doctor said that it was as if you were in some sort of hibernation and they thought it best for you to wake up naturally."

Again his dad paused before continuing. "I was so worried; I couldn't really take in what they were saying. When I went to see you and your mum, you were snuggled in the crook of her arm and wrapped in a soft, baby blanket. There were two midwives there. I don't know what we would have done without those two, lovely women. They were so calm and reassuring.

They encouraged us to talk to you, to welcome you and tell you how much you were wanted and loved. If it wasn't for them, I think I would have just sat there in shock and not said a word." Alex's dad shook his head as if he still could not believe it, then he went on with the story. "They gave us the words to say and showed us how to stroke your face and head so you could feel the gentleness of our touch and be aware that we were there for you.

They treated the situation as if it was quite normal and that helped us to calm down. You began to move one of your hands a little and I gave you my little finger to hold. I was surprised at how strong your grip was seeing that you were still fast asleep."

After a final swig of his now cold tea, Alex's dad carried on. "Tears were streaming down your mum's face as she kept pleading for you to wake up. After what seemed like hours, there was no further change. Your mum was exhausted.

The midwives came in closer and one put her hand on your head and the other one put her hand on your chest. They smiled at us and at each other and then spoke to you very gently. They told you that everything was okay and that you would not be alone. They then told you it was time to wake up. With that, you suddenly opened your eyes wide and smiled at them and then at us. It was as if nothing had been wrong at all.

The doctors couldn't understand it at all, but the midwives just explained that you needed more time than others to adjust. They stayed a while longer to make sure that we were all okay and when they went, all three of us fell asleep."

His dad reached over and gave Alex a quick hug. "We were so relieved and thankful when you finally woke up and seemed so happy. After scaring the life out of us, you were a healthy and contented baby. We felt then that we were blessed to have you, and we still do," he added.

Alex had never heard this story before. It was extraordinary. He was really pleased that his dad had shared it with him. It also made him realise how special he was to his parents.

"Do you know who the two midwives were?" asked Alex.

"Sadly, no," he replied. "I never saw the midwives again, but if ever I meet them, I would give them a big hug because I am so grateful to them. They were just such lovely people."

They sat quietly for a while, each of them thinking about the story of his birth. Then Alex's dad stood up and stretched. He bent to ruffle Willow's back. He threw her a bit of bread and then began to gather his tools and gloves.

Unexpectedly, he sat back down and added a bit more to the story.

"Three months after you were born, I went to answer a knock at the door. There was no one there, which was strange as we have such a long drive at the front of the house. On the doorstep, I found a dog basket with a note tied to the handle, a bag of dog food and a bag with toys, a lead and collar. Inside the basket, was a tiny, soft, furry ball, an adorable puppy which was curled up and fast asleep. The note said, *'THIS IS WILLOW AND SHE IS A GIFT TO ALEX'*.

When I picked her up and looked into her beautiful, brown eyes, I just knew we had to keep her. There was something so special about her."

He lent forward and cupped Willow's face in his big hands and looked into her eyes. Then he sat stroking her. "From the minute she arrived, she never let you out of her sight and followed you around, even at bath time, as if she was guarding you. Willow was not at all interested in the rest of us, although she would let us pet and stroke her. She was your dog and yours alone."

Alex was fascinated. All this amazing new information was making this a birthday to remember.

His dad went off to the shed and got out the lawnmower while Alex cleared the lunch things away. He mowed the back lawn and then went to water the tomatoes and lettuces in the greenhouse.

Then, together they went through the house to the front, carrying the lawnmower between them so as not to scuff the walls in the hallway.

While his dad mowed the front lawn, Alex made a start on weeding the flowerbeds. He always found weeding very satisfying and there was often a pleasant surprise when he found a lovely plant or two which had been hidden in amongst all the weeds.

As for most things, Alex had a system for gardening. There had to be a start, middle and an end to every job and everything had to be done in order. Also, he liked to tidy as he went along. He would never leave everything to clear away at the end.

He decided he would start the weeding at the bottom right hand side of the garden near no. 15's fence. Then he would continue in a clockwise direction until he arrived back to where he had started. He fetched a bucket and began. He pulled out the longest weeds first as he found them much easier to pull out with their roots still attached.

By the time he had cleared a small patch of the flowerbed, he had already filled the bucket with weeds and went off to empty it onto the compost heap at the back. As he walked down the back garden, he took in the lovely smell of freshly mown grass.

His dad had finished the front lawn and had wheeled the lawnmower back through the house on his own. He was now using the garden spade to make the edges of the back lawn look neat and tidy. It was very pleasing to look at and Alex complimented his dad.

When Alex returned to the front garden, there was a woman standing by the fence at no. 15. She was tall and slim and had the whitest, shoulder length, curly hair he had ever seen and beautiful blue eyes. She was dressed in a plain, long, white dress. She raised her hand to wave and called to Alex. He could hear that odd humming sound again. She called him by his name. He was surprised that she knew his name as he was sure he had never seen her before. Intrigued, he went closer to the fence. She smiled as she introduced herself.

"My name is Marguerite Judge but, as we are now next door neighbours, you can just call me Marguerite."

Even though she had used his name already, Alex still felt the need to introduce himself properly and he gave her his little speech.

"I'm the middle one of three Angels and my name is Alexander Noah Angel." He also added, "As we are now next door neighbours, you can just call me Alex."

She smiled at him again. Alex sensed that she was a really sincere, kind person too, just like Poppy at no.13.

"It is really nice to see you again. I look forward to catching up with you soon," she said and then turned, walked quickly away and disappeared inside her house.

Alex thought it really peculiar that the two women, who had only just moved in either side of his house, thought they already knew him. Maybe it was a case of mistaken identity. That would be awkward. What were they going to catch up about and when and where was it going to take place?

He stood looking after Marguerite and then noticed how her garden had changed. The big circular bed was now full of beautiful, white calla lilies, not quite in full bloom. They really stood out against the green of the grass. He marvelled at the stripes on the lawn too. Where it had been trimmed so neatly, it was like a bowling green.

The rest of the afternoon was spent clearing all four of the flowerbeds bordering the narrow, rectangular lawn at the front. Alex stood back and surveyed his work when he had finished and felt very pleased with what he had achieved.

With the last bucket of weeds on the compost heap, his dad produced a large net of daffodil bulbs and a couple of packets of seeds. Together, they planted them in the newly cleared flowerbeds in the front garden as planned.

The light began to fade so they went indoors for another well-earned mug of tea.

Alex's dad decided to have a bath while Alex went to his bedroom. He looked out of his window just in case Marguerite and Poppy were out there, but there was no sign of them.

He curled up on his bed and curled himself around Willow's back, thinking about his new neighbours, where they had come from and why they thought they knew him. He wondered what they would be doing right now. This made him jump up, as he suddenly realised that what *he* should be doing now, was taking Willow out for her walk before it got completely dark.

When they got back from their walk, Willow had her dinner and a drink and Alex made himself two cheese and pickle sandwiches on white bread. Alex was glad that neither of his brothers was at home tonight. It meant that he could eat his dinner without the fear of being put off it. If his brothers were home at the weekend, they would sometimes wait until he went into the front room to eat and then they would deliberately either pick their noses or break wind in front of him, which put him right off his food. Whenever they did this, Alex always got really upset, but they just laughed it off.

His mum had got back from work while he was out walking with Willow. She and his dad were already ensconced on the smaller sofa in the front room, watching 'On the Buses' on the television.

Alex carried his sandwiches and strawberry drink in and sprawled out on the longer sofa with his companion next to him.

"Hello Love, happy birthday! Have you enjoyed your day? I must say, the front garden is looking so much better. Thank you, my birthday boy. Come and give me a kiss."

Alex went over for a birthday kiss and hug.

"What about me?" his dad wanted to know. "I worked hard too, you know!" He nudged her and puckered up for a kiss.

She laughed.

"Get away with you! You're not my special birthday boy! Have you had a good day, Alex?"

"Yes thanks, and thank you so much for the lovely books. We looked up some bits today as we were gardening. They're great. I'm getting quite a reference library now.

I met both the new neighbours today. The one at no. 13's called Poppy Longate and the other one's called Marguerite Judge. They're really friendly. Did you see their gardens? They're already looking beautiful."

"I noticed the front gardens. I wonder how they did it all so quickly when your dad finds it so hard to keep on top of his."

His dad did not appreciate the dig at him. He laughed as he said, "At least we've got vegetables picked from our garden for Sunday lunch. I don't think you'd appreciate a bowl of flowers for dinner!"

Alex's mum went to the kitchen to make some tea. She shouted out, "The back garden looks fantastic! Thank you BOTH!"

She returned, balancing a small sponge cake and plates in one hand and two mugs of tea in the other. Alex jumped up and rescued the cake and plates and put them on the table.

She had sprinkled icing sugar on the top of the cake and had put in loads of extra strawberry jam so it was oozing out of the middle. She had already cut it into three, chunky slices. Alex's mum handed him one of the slices on a plate.

"Happy birthday, my special boy!"

Alex took a big bite of his slice of cake and delighted in the sensation of the jam squishing through his teeth.

"Delicious! Thank you." His words were muffled by the sponge and jam, but his mum smiled with pleasure at his obvious enjoyment.

Alex really looked forward to having a lovely, relaxing evening with just him, Willow and his parents. This was a lovely present. There was another bonus too as 'Doctor Who' was on as well. Tom Baker had recently started as the new Doctor and Alex really liked him.

Chapter 14

Although Alex tried to hang on to his special birthday time for a while longer, his eyes eventually closed and with a last, big sigh, he was fast asleep and, almost immediately, found himself back in the beautiful garden. It was blissful. The fragrances were wonderful.

As he walked through the garden, gently brushing the flowers with the tips of his outstretched fingers, he heard the sound of far off voices. He stopped and listened.

Then, in the distance, he saw two people walking towards him. They were side by side and there seemed to be a shimmering glow above them. He waited as they came closer. One of them was wearing a pair of trousers and a top covered in a bright pattern of large, exotic multi-coloured flowers and the other was wearing a plain, long, white dress.

It was Poppy and Marguerite, but with wings!

Alex was confused and wondered how they came to be in his dream. Who were they really? The two women smiled warmly at him.

Marguerite spoke first. "We are both so happy to see you as we have been looking forward to speaking to you again."

Alex was none the wiser.

"I don't know if you had guessed it yet but, Poppy and I were the midwives present at your birth, exactly thirteen years ago today!"

"You were such a perfect, beautiful baby," Poppy told him.

Alex still felt bewildered. Then he recalled what his dad had told him earlier in the garden.

"From the moment you were born, we followed how you developed and grew," continued Poppy.

Alex stared at them in disbelief. He could not understand how they could have done this. Surely he would have been aware that he was being followed or spied on.

They could see that he was struggling to understand how this was possible.

"You see," said Marguerite, "we are angels."

Alex laughed nervously.

Marguerite added, "I am an angel of truth and honesty."

Poppy said, "And I am an angel of all growing things."

The idea that angels had been watching him all his life was difficult for Alex to conceive. They knew he needed more information to help him make sense of this news, so Marguerite began to tell him the story of his unusual birth.

"You had everyone worried when you were born because you were fast asleep. You just did not seem ready to wake up straight away."

Alex was taken by surprise to hear this from Marguerite as he had only just found this out today from his dad. Had she been listening when his dad told him the story of his birth in the garden earlier?

Poppy then explained, "Before you were born, you had been chosen to receive a special gift which would carry responsibility. You were told that you would meet many tough challenges in your life, but that you would be given the strength to persevere. No matter how difficult things became, you were told that the purpose of your gift would become clearer and easier to manage."

Marguerite continued, "The message was a bit overwhelming for you. So, before you were born, you went into a kind of human hibernation. You did not feel ready to start on your new journey of life."

"As you were lying there, asleep in your mother's arms," Poppy carried on, "we both reassured you that everything would be okay because you would not be alone. Your parents probably remember us telling you this and also that it was okay for you to wake up. It was when you heard our voices that you opened your eyes wide and smiled at us and then at your parents. Everyone was so relieved and happy."

It was the same story his dad had told him, but Poppy had not been in her garden so how could she know this bit ... unless she was actually there at his birth? It was difficult for Alex to take in all of this.

Poppy went on with the story. "Three months after your birth, we placed a tiny puppy in a dog basket along with a note and a few necessities on the front doorstep of where your family lived. Willow was given to you because she is a special guardian dog. She was sent to watch over you and to be your friend when things got difficult. You have always had someone watching over you and you have never been alone."

Alex sat down abruptly among the flowers to think. He weighed it all up and decided that he was being told the truth, however implausible it seemed. Things were beginning to fall into place but there was so much he still did not understand.

He had a real sense of how true and honest Marguerite and Poppy were and felt that he could trust them. What they said gave him a warm and comforted feeling, but he had so many questions. What was his 'special gift'? Why him? What challenges? How were they going to help him?

Together, the two angels tried to give him more reassurance and answers to his questions.

"We have watched you grow into a kind, thoughtful and gentle boy," said Marguerite. "We

are so proud of the way you have conducted
yourself when things have been difficult. We can
see that, although you find it hard being different,
you do not take the easy way out and allow others
to lead you astray, just to fit in."

Poppy went on to say, "We are especially proud
that you do not argue or fight and that you have a
very clear sense of what is right. You always try
to follow the path of truth."

Alex felt a glow of pride as he listened.

"We are here to help you with the situations
you are dealing with at the moment," Marguerite
explained. "We have been observing Scott,
Harvey, Jimmy, Tommy and Lee. The way you
have handled their behaviour towards you is
admirable. However, you now need a bit of help
because, unfortunately, those boys will find it
really hard to see the error of their ways without
some special intervention. Lee is going to be your
first assignment."

Alex wondered what they would do to help and
what did they mean by 'assignment'? It was
beginning to feel very scary.

"Don't worry," Poppy reassured him. "It will all
become clear to you in due course and you will
have our full support."

They both put their hands lightly on his
shoulders which made him feel really safe and
protected. He stood up and pulled his shoulders
back as he felt a strong surge of empowerment. He
did not feel alone now.

They continued walking through the garden.

"There will be changes from Monday," said Poppy. "Some of the things you see will seem very strange, but you must not be frightened. Another important thing is that you must resist the urge to talk to anyone about what you see and what you know about us. You can carry on confiding in Willow, of course." They laughed.

Alex laughed too as he realised they knew he had a habit of talking to Willow when he was upset or anxious.

He loved the idea that Willow was his 'special guardian dog'. He always thought that she was special, but now he felt that she was super special. He was amazed that he was in the company of angels and that Marguerite and Poppy were sent to help him, but he still felt really unsure of what they were expecting him to do and how they would help him.

Just as Alex was about to ask what they meant by 'assignment', he experienced that strange feeling of being pulled backwards. The garden receded as if he were in a fast, rewinding film. Everything became blurred and voices indistinct. He desperately wanted to stay, but was powerless to resist. Just on the edge of his consciousness, he became aware of a familiar sound. It became louder and more insistent.

"Alex! Alex!" she called and shook him lightly.

His eyes snapped open and there, bending over him, was his mum.

Nicola Hedges

"Oh! Thank goodness you've woken up," she said as she flumped on the sofa with relief. "I was so worried. I thought you would never wake up, just like when you were a baby."

Alex struggled to sit up and gave his mum a reassuring hug.

It was Sunday morning and eleven o'clock already. Last night, he had fallen asleep on the sofa with his dog by his side. His parents had put a blanket over him to keep him warm during the night as they thought it was best to leave him where he was so that he could get a good night's sleep.

Alex rubbed his eyes. He was still not quite awake. The line between reality and dream was very blurred. The dream he had just had did not feel like a dream at all. It really was as if he had been in that beautiful garden with Marguerite and Poppy. He almost wished that he was there still.

Willow nudged Alex several times until, feeling a bit more alert, he staggered upstairs to get washed and changed.

He caught sight of his reflection in the mirror as he undressed and saw the newly formed scabs covering the grazes on his knees, a fist sized bruise on his upper arm and a bruise on his shin. He dressed quickly and hoped that he would not acquire any more 'decorations' like these.

Chapter 15

Down in the kitchen, his mum was sitting at the table on her own, reading the newspaper and drinking a cup of tea as she did every Sunday morning.

Alex moved around quietly, putting the porridge on to cook and saw to Willow's needs. Then he sat in his place and ate in silence. His mum was engrossed in one of the newspaper stories. He tried to get his brain in gear.

It was Sunday, car cleaning day. His dad had an old Austin Cambridge. He had scrimped and saved and bought a second hand one before Scott was born as he did not want to be caught out again if there were any problems with the birth as there had been with Alex.

Alex loved the burgundy and cream colours and the pointed tail lights which he thought looked like rockets.

His dad had some special cream in a tube and a soft cloth to buff up all the chrome – the emblem, the name like a signature, the trim, the bumpers, hub caps, mirrors and grill at the front. Alex liked doing these bits best. Seeing his distorted image in the back of the wing mirrors made him laugh.

There was also an old, out of date, car recovery badge stuck on the back window.

He fetched a bucket from the shed; half filled it with warm water, added a little car cleaning liquid and wafted his hand about in the water to create some foam. Bucket in one hand and polish and rags in the other, he went out to make a start on his dad's mud spattered car.

Alex was squatting behind the car to clean the back bumper and number plate when Willow started to growl. Alex froze for a moment as he heard Lee calling him. He straightened up slowly to look at him.

Lee was smiling. It looked a little false. He gestured Alex over with his head and called out that he had something he really wanted to show him.

Reassuring his dog, who was still growling, Alex slowly walked towards Lee. He hoped that he would behave himself as he was right outside Alex's home.

Even from a distance, Alex could see that Lee's hands were cupped together, concealing something. His heart sank. He knew there was a poor creature trapped inside those cruel hands.

"Don't look so worried, Alex!" Lee called out. "I found something in the bush around the corner I thought you might like to see. I'm being ever so gentle."

Alex walked up to the front gate and leant over the top of it. Lee slowly parted his hands just enough for Alex to see what it was, but not wide enough for whatever it was to escape. As Alex peered into the gap, he thought that he would see some poor, mutilated creature. He was surprised and relieved when he saw a lovely, little butterfly which was in one piece and still alive. Alex smiled and thought that maybe Lee had turned over a new leaf. But, quick as a flash, Lee pinched the butterfly wings together, bent down and placed it under one of his shoes and twisted his foot exaggeratedly while he grinned malevolently at Alex.

Alex reeled back in shock and cried out as if in pain. He could not believe his eyes. How could Lee do that? How could he be so utterly cruel? Red hot anger bubbled up inside him and, before he knew it, he was standing face to face with Lee, looking him straight in the eye and shouting.

"What's wrong with you? You're a cruel, senseless idiot! How could you?"

Lee's face twisted with hatred. He lunged towards Alex over the gate and managed to get a firm grip on a fistful of his hair and then started to twist. It was agony.

Willow shot along the driveway, barking and growling fiercely. She flung herself at the gate and snapped at Lee's arm, but she could not quite reach.

Suddenly, Lee released his grip and just stood there on the pavement. At the same time, Alex heard the, by now, familiar, humming and a woman's voice call Lee's name. The dog continued to growl.

Alex gently touched his head and found that it was bleeding. There was a clump of his hair on the drive in front of him. What just happened? As Alex looked around, he saw both Marguerite and Poppy standing at their front gates. He realised that they had probably witnessed the whole thing.

"Hello Lee," said Marguerite. "Come over here a minute."

Alex was surprised when Lee did as she asked.

"What happened to the butterfly?" she asked him gently.

Lee laughed. "It's not going to be flying anywhere soon!"

Marguerite looked very sad. "You have caused pain to a beautiful creature and destroyed it. That was a cruel and senseless thing to do. Choosing something so delicate, small and defenceless to destroy when you are like a giant to it makes you a coward," she explained.

Lee looked a bit embarrassed but his old bravado soon returned. "I don't care," he told her. "Anyway, you should mind your own business!"

Poppy came out onto the pavement and walked over to Lee.

"Why did you attack Alex? He is much smaller than you and he was right to be upset by what you just did."

"Oh, get knotted!" said Lee belligerently. "You all need to watch out and don't stick your noses in my business. I'll do whatever I like and you can't stop me."

"You need to understand that if you do not change your ways, there will be consequences for your actions," Poppy replied.

Lee laughed. "I couldn't care less what two old biddies think!" He turned on his heel and strutted off up the hill.

Alex was pleased that Marguerite and Poppy had challenged Lee's behaviour, but felt disappointed that he had reacted so rudely towards them. He also wondered what it would mean for him back at school. His head really smarted.

"Thank you for being helpful. I don't know what it is with Lee, but he always seems to take delight in destroying any little creature he finds. It's so upsetting." Alex rubbed his head gingerly. He seemed to be collecting a lot of 'war wounds' in a short space of time.

Marguerite and Poppy smiled warmly at Alex.

"That is what we are here for," said Poppy.

Marguerite winked at him. "Remember, we really are angels and things will start to get better from tomorrow, promise."

Alex beamed when he heard this. He felt so happy to know that his 'dream' was, in fact, real and that the angels had come to help him. He was not sure what they could do when he was at school though, but he tried not to worry.

As Alex went back to finish washing the car, Willow jumped up and down alongside him. She was so glad he was safe. Alex gave her lots of strokes and cuddles. She had been such a brave, little dog.

Alex picked up a dry rag and polish to give the car a final shine. He paused to look at his neighbours' front gardens. Poppy's flowerbeds were full of beautiful, pink flowers which were now in full bloom and the large, circular flowerbed in the middle of Marguerite's lawn was crammed full of bright, white calla lilies which were now open.

Alex felt that there really was something other worldly about his new neighbours and felt very lucky to have them on his side.

When he had given the last buff to the car, Alex put everything away and got his dad to come out and give his verdict.

"Missed a bit!" his dad joked.

Alex was disappointed and scanned the bodywork for the offending area.

"I'm only teasing," his dad laughed. "You've done a grand job! Thank you." He was, in fact, very pleased because Alex was always so thorough. He gave Alex a hug as he handed him his well-earned fifty pence.

Alex ran straight upstairs to his room, shut the door, lay on his stomach and wriggled part way under the bed and popped the money into his 'puppy bank'. He made sure it was well hidden again. Only Willow knew about his secret hoard.

Sunday lunch was just being served up, including sweetcorn and runner beans from the garden, when he bounced into the kitchen.

From his usual place at the end of the table, Alex asked his parents, "Have you met our new neighbours yet?"

"No," they both replied in unison.

"I've chatted to them both now and they're really friendly and kind. We're very lucky to have such lovely people living next door to us." He really wanted to tell them something of what he knew about their new neighbours, but he had promised not to.

"Perhaps we'll catch them later today," said his dad.

After lunch, Alex cleared away and washed up and then it was time to walk his dog. They trotted up the hill to Greenleah Heights. They ran, played fetch and chase together. When they were both tired and out of breath, they collapsed on the grass.

Alex began to think out loud to Willow about all the strange, new information he had been given, his 'dreams' and his encounter with Lee earlier. He really did not know what to think.

Willow kept looking at him with her head on one side and her ears attentive. When he finished, she reached out one of her paws and put it on his hand as if to let him know that she understood. Then the wind started to pick up, making them shiver, so they ran all the way home down the hill.

Collar and lead off and hands washed, Alex sought the refuge of his bedroom. It had been a tiring couple of days and it was a school day tomorrow. He shook his beanbag before sagging into it. He reached for one of the books he had been given for his birthday, the one about insects.

It always filled Alex with wonder that so many tiny creatures had such intricate features and beautiful markings. He often thought the explanation for their presence could not be entirely due to chance. Willow was curled up beside Alex and every so often, he stroked her head and rubbed her ears as he read.

Several hours later, Alex's mum shouted out that dinner was ready.

First, Alex gave the dog her food and a fresh bowl of water and then he went and sat in his usual chair to have his dinner.

Harvey and Scott were back now and were full of tales of what they had got up to, vying with each other to describe who had the best time. Alex just sat quietly and listened. He thought that his weekend knocked spots off theirs!

When they had finished talking, Alex was able to get their attention.

"I just want to say thank you for the lovely presents you gave Willow. She likes the treats and is pleased to have a new tennis ball as the old one was getting a bit manky."

"Hmmm," Harvey grunted in acknowledgment.

"It's okay," mumbled Scott.

After dinner, Harvey went upstairs first to have his weekly bath. It would be Scott's turn next and then Alex's. Alex always had his bath last. He finished helping his mum to clear everything away in the kitchen and then she started doing the ironing.

Alex and Willow went into the front room where his dad was asleep in front of the television. He really wanted to talk to his dad in private so the others would not make fun of him. He knew he only had a small window of opportunity before they were disturbed, so he decided to wake him. Once he was awake, Alex asked him the questions that had been burning in his mind.

"Dad, do you believe that angels exist? What do you think about them?"

Alex's dad was rather surprised by these questions as they seemed to come out of the blue.

"I firmly believe that angels exist," he began. "I think that they are everywhere. People don't take the time to notice them, but they are there and they are wonderful." Then he added, "I believe the two midwives at your birth were angels because they just knew what to do and say to help you and me and your mum."

Alex thought his dad was very perceptive. He really wanted to tell him just how right he was. It was hard for him to be unable to share what he knew with his dad.

Their conversation came to an abrupt end when Alex heard Scott shouting down the stairs that it was his turn to have a bath. He quickly thanked his dad and then made his way up the stairs.

In the bathroom, the floor was littered with Scott's damp towel and dirty clothes, as usual. Without saying a word, Alex hung the towel on the hook, scooped up the rest of the clothes, and put them into the washing basket on the landing.

When he returned to the bathroom, he looked down at the bath water with dismay. It was very murky. Alex assumed that his brothers must have been covered in mud before they had their bath. He had a strong urge to pull the plug out, wash the bath round and then fill it up with lovely, hot, clean water just for himself. He hated having to share the bath water, but he was told it was a 'necessity'.

As he reluctantly lowered himself into the bath, the coolness of the water hit him. That just added insult to injury! Alex was determined that he would make this bath experience as brief as possible.

Afterwards, he dried himself briskly with his towel, brushed his teeth, cleared his stuff away and hurried back to his room.

Alex got into bed. Willow woke up and decided she would move higher up the bed so he could cuddle her as he read his new birthday book about insects. He started reading the chapter about ants. He carefully studied the magnified sections of the photographs. The details were amazing. He read for about an hour before he was overcome with tiredness, fell asleep and travelled back to the beautiful garden.

It was a perfect day. The sky was a pale shade of blue and the sun was shining down. As he strolled along the garden path, he stopped several times to smell the different flowers. He felt totally at ease and comfortable there. The scent of the flowers made him feel sleepy so he wandered off the path and found a grassy bank where he sat watching the butterflies and gently drifted off into an even deeper sleep.

Chapter 16

The following morning, Alex woke up well before everyone else. He got out of bed with a smile on his face and felt unusually happy.

It was Monday and he was actually looking forward to going to school because he knew that today was the day that things were going to start to change, even though he did not know how.

As he pulled his bedroom curtains open wide, the pale morning light crept into the room. He looked out of his window and saw Marguerite and Poppy's beautiful gardens with his own well maintained one in the middle. He sighed with contentment and thought how lucky he was.

He made his bed and then went into the bathroom. He took his time as there was no one to hassle him to be quick because they were all still asleep. It felt good.

Alex and Willow bounced downstairs for breakfast. He decided to make the porridge for everyone. Willow's food had disappeared quickly so he let her out into the garden. He made the porridge runny, just the way he liked it. He opened his book about insects to read as he slowly ate his porridge.

It was still early and getting brighter by the minute. He thought he would walk around the block with his four legged friend before school. He left a note by the kettle to say where he was in case they worried that he was not around.

Outside, there was a misty halo around the street lamps, although the sun was beginning to peep from behind the hill. Alex breathed in deeply, taking in the smell of freshly cut grass. He loved that smell because it reminded him of white marquees pitched on luscious, green grass on a beautiful, hot, sunny day. He thought that maybe it was linked to a distant, happy memory from a camping holiday in North Devon when he was much younger.

Willow trotted by Alex's side. She stopped every now and then to sniff where other dogs had been. Alex was happy to follow her leisurely pace as there was still plenty of time.

The neighbourhood was coming to life. There were lights on in some houses and the sound of voices and radios drifted out into the crisp air. Cars started up and heels clacked along the pavement as people traipsed off for the bus stop or work. Often Alex's dad would be up and out too at this time, but he had a later start today.

Alex was getting cold so he began to jog back with his funny little mutt bouncing along on the end of her lead. They were both out of breath as they dashed into the kitchen.

"Thanks for making the porridge, my love," his mum said. "It means I don't have such a rush today."

"I'm glad you left that note, Alex, otherwise I would have thought that the fairies had spirited you away in the night," teased his dad.

Harvey, on the other hand, put a dampener on things. "Shame about the runny porridge though, some of us would prefer not to have soup for breakfast!"

"Harvey!" both parents remonstrated.

Alex held his tongue and decided he would go to school on his own again today as he was ready anyway, rather than have to put up with Harvey's bad mood. He hurriedly said goodbye to them all and gave Willow a few strokes at the front door before setting off up the hill.

He was surprised at how many other children were out this early. He guessed they wanted to meet up with friends. He wished he had a group of friends or even just one in his class. He sighed and began to think about how his day at school would be. He could not help peering around in case Jimmy, Tommy or Lee was about.

In the 'dream' garden, the angels had previously made it very clear that changes were going to happen and he was excited, but also a little scared, as he had no idea what this really meant.

The playground was already crowded and noisy. He felt uncomfortable, but he did well and managed to avoid covering his ears up. He walked away from the noisiest area and made for the grassy bank and his favourite oak tree. He put his hand on the trunk and waited until he could feel the life force surging under his hand. He looked up into the branches and felt quite humbled by the tree's beauty. He remembered that there were oak trees in his 'dream' garden too and this was comforting.

Alex needed to use the toilet before school started. He really wished that he had remembered to go before leaving home, but Harvey had put him off his stroke. He hated the toilet block.

He peered into the gloom and his heart sank as Lee was there at the sink again. It was just Alex, Lee and a poor beetle he had caught.

Lee was hunched over, toying with the beetle. He watched it as it tried to escape. Each time it managed to get to the edge of his hand, he flicked it so that it tumbled back into his palm. The poor thing must have been exhausted.

Alex knew that Lee was not going to let it go. Very soon, he would start pulling the beetle's legs off, one by one, just as he had with the daddy longlegs, or crush it under his foot as he had done with the beautiful butterfly. Alex shuddered at the thought and decided that he was not going to let him do it this time. Not again.

"Stop it Lee!" he called out, in a voice much stronger than he felt. "That beetle has feelings and it's much smaller than you. You're just being cruel!" He then asked him, "How would you feel if what you're doing to it happened to you?"

Lee ignored Alex. Just as he was about to pull a leg off, it was as if there was a tremendous surge of energy in the room. Alex was slammed against the cold, rough wall. The knobbles of thick paint pressed into his skin painfully. What had just happened? Why was it so dark all of a sudden?

Then he saw it. An absolutely enormous beetle! It towered over Lee, who was now cowering and barely visible beneath it.

Alex could see the segmented body, the textured stripes on its wing casings, the joints and claws on each of its legs. The lights were reflected in the many lenses of its compound eyes, making it appear to be looking in all directions at once. Its spikey antlers scraped and rattled on the walls.

The beetle filled most of the space as it reared up on its back legs. It was like a scene from a scary movie. At first, Alex felt really frightened. He stayed as still as he could and then eased himself away from the wall.

He remembered that the angels had told him strange things would happen, and this was certainly right up there. He could now hear the humming he had grown to associate with them.

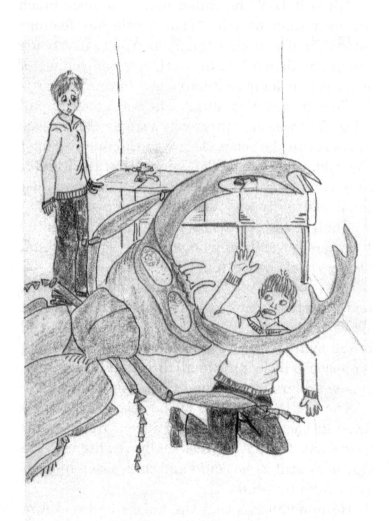

He realised that the beetle was not interested in him. As Alex stared in wonder and horror, the beetle gripped hold of one of Lee's arms with its mandibles. Lee looked absolutely terrified. The beetle tugged at his arm.

"Let go! Get off me! Let me go! Let me go!" Lee pleaded. But it carried on, pulling his arm just a tiny bit more each time until Lee was almost hanging by his arm. "Help! Heeeelp!" he shouted.

Alex knew that this was the work of the angels and did not like to interfere.

Lee struggled and tried to get his arm out of the beetle's grip, but it would not let him go. When he started to scream hysterically, Alex instinctively darted forward to help. The beetle suddenly let him go and Lee fell sprawling on to the floor. He scrambled up and, clutching his arm, staggered out of the building. He belted across the playground.

"Help! Help! There's a monster! Help! It's trying to kill me!" he yelled hysterically.

Alex watched in fascination as the enormous beetle shrank back to its normal size and scurried down a hole in the concrete floor.

Several minutes later, a group of excited children pushed and shoved at the entrance of the toilet block.

"Let's have a look. Where's this monster then?" one of the children asked.

"What if it gets us?" another said, feeling scared.

As Alex was washing his hands, he noticed that there was a wet patch on the floor by the sink where Lee had been standing. Alex calmly dried his hands and went towards the exit.

The children shrieked as he emerged, thinking that they had spotted the monster. They fell over each other in their excitement. When they regrouped, they rushed towards Alex.

"Where is it?"

"Did you see it?"

"Where's the monster?" they shouted.

Alex looked at them with a surprised expression. "What monster are you on about?" he asked them. He thought that the only 'monster' he had seen in the toilets was Lee. "There's no monster here. Have a look for yourselves." He invited them in. Then, with a knowing look, he left as they went to investigate.

Crossing the playground with his head held high, Alex saw Lee sitting on a bench. He was crying; his face was pale; he was shaking and looked really shocked. One of the boys sitting next to him wrapped his arm around his shoulder to try to comfort him. Another went to get a member of staff.

Then the group of children, who had gone to seek out the monster, ran back to the bench where Lee was.

"You're a liar, liar, pants on fire!" several of the children jeered.

"There's no monster anywhere!" They laughed at him.

"You're just a chicken!" they taunted.

"Off you go now. I don't want to hear any name calling, thank you very much," said the dinner lady who had been brought to take care of Lee. She sat down next to him as the children dispersed.

With everyone's attention elsewhere, Alex was able to get into school and down to the end of the corridor without being set upon.

He sat thoughtfully on the floor. As he waited, he replayed the sequence of events. The whole thing was surreal! How on earth had the beetle suddenly become so big?

Although it was awful to see Lee in such a state, Alex thought that it may have been a dramatic and unforgettable lesson for him. At least now, he should have some insight into how all the insects he had ill-treated must have felt, and how utterly wrong his behaviour had been.

Alex felt quite disturbed by what he had seen. Something strange and powerful had occurred and he was connected to it in some way.

His classmates were full of versions of what had happened. They talked about 'the monster in the toilet building' and 'the boy who had wet himself'. The children were making fun of Lee. Alex felt very uncomfortable with this.

Everyone was talking at once and making scary monster sounds. It made Alex's head hurt. He quickly got his notebook and pen out and began writing a list of insects and all their characteristics, to block out the noise while he waited for Mr Dear to arrive and restore order.

Mr Dear took the register. They had not even been back a whole week yet and already there were two children absent.

As they got settled in the hall, Alex focussed again on what Mr Adams was saying. The message seemed to be about doing one's best when it came to learning. Alex did not think the message was meant for him today as he knew he was already doing his best. He thought that it was probably aimed at children like Harvey and Scott because they definitely did not do their best.

Alex went off to the art room for his first lesson. He felt happy as he walked along because he enjoyed art. However, there was a new teacher called Mrs Bartlett. Alex was a little anxious as he had never met her before. He studied her face as he entered the classroom. He did not think it looked very welcoming. In fact, he thought she looked positively unfriendly and did not warm to her at all! He aimed for a seat at the back of the classroom but, as he did so, she stopped him.

"No! No! I don't think so! I would like you to sit over there." She pointed to one of the desks right at the front of the class.

"Sorry, Mrs Bartlett," he stuttered, feeling very distressed. "I need to sit at the back. I can't sit at the front. I mean it makes it very difficult for me if I sit there."

Even some of the children told her that Alex always sat at the back which surprised him. She would not listen, so Alex did as he was told. He found it just a bit too much on top of the weird start to the day.

Mrs Bartlett brought round a bowl of fruit for them to look at and then placed it on a high stool. Next, she showed them a variety of posters with bowls of fruit depicted by famous artists. They were in watercolour, acrylic, pen and ink; some looked like photos while others were really weird shapes and colours and looked nothing like any fruit Alex had seen.

Art paper was handed out. He did not really know what she was expecting them to do. He tried to focus on the bowl of fruit. He picked up a pencil and began to sketch, but tears trickled down his cheeks and onto the piece of paper in front of him.

He could not see what the others were doing. If only she knew how unnecessarily difficult she was making things for him. Alex had to resist an overwhelming desire to run out of the classroom. He kept his head down and concentrated on the shapes of the fruit and the way the light fell on the bowl. He began to calm down, but wanted reassurance that he was on the right track. Throughout the lesson, the teacher went round the class, offering feedback and help. She did not look at Alex's work so he felt that she was pointedly ignoring him. He felt miserable.

When the bell went, Alex was the first one out of the room. He was angry as he felt that his enjoyment of art was spoilt. He used to be good at art, but now he was floundering and felt stupid and embarrassed. What a morning!

Chapter 17

Small motes of dust danced in the sunlight as it shone through the corridor windows. Alex held his face up to the light and closed his eyes briefly. He enjoyed the mottled pink and purple colours of his eyelids and the warmth on his face.

Someone bumped into him as he stood in the middle of the corridor. He quickly opened his eyes and decided to go outside to have his lunch. He needed to go to the toilet before he ate, but the cloakroom was heaving with children and there was a queue for the toilets. He could not bear the racket in there so he would have to go to the toilet block outside. He was fairly confident that Lee would not put in an appearance after his earlier experience.

It was completely empty so he slipped into one of the cubicles. When he came out a few minutes later, the building was still empty. He washed his hands and allowed himself to relax a little, but then he became aware of movement by the entrance.

He looked up and there was Lee! Alex's heart started to beat faster. Lee came towards him. Alex backed away until he was jammed up against the sinks. Lee had that familiar, cruel look on his face.

"It's all your fault!" he shouted. "Everyone's making fun of me."

"But I never did anything to you," Alex protested. "Anyway, you were warned to stop being cruel to insects or face the consequences."

"Shut up! Just shut up!" Lee said through gritted teeth.

He clenched his right fist as tightly as he could, making his knuckles turn white. He pulled his arm back sharply before driving it forward with all the speed and strength he could manage, aiming straight at Alex's stomach. Alex closed his eyes, anticipating the impact of Lee's fist with dread. He winced as he heard a loud thud and then an agonised groan.

But Alex felt no pain. Confused, he opened his eyes. Everything looked different. He wondered what had happened. He looked around.

His back was now touching the ceiling and he had to bend his neck to avoid the light fitting pressing against the sore patch on his head. His body was bent like the letter 'L'. The humming was back. He must be at least twenty feet tall now!

Lee was in a heap on the floor in tears, rocking back and forth as he nursed his right hand. He was obviously in considerable pain.

It suddenly dawned on Alex that just as Lee was going to punch him in the stomach, he must have morphed into a long, skinny giant and Lee would have hit the sink in between his long, bandy legs instead of his stomach. Alex was very glad that he had not been hit again.

Lee was too preoccupied to notice Alex's body slowly return to normal. Alex felt a bit unsteady, but he calmly picked up his satchel and went to find a dinner lady.

"Lee's in the toilets. He's hurt his hand. It might be broken. He's crying with the pain," he told her. It was the same lady who had helped Lee before.

"Don't tell me the monster finally got him!" she exclaimed sarcastically.

"He's really badly hurt," repeated Alex.

"Humph! Anyone would think I had no other children to keep an eye on!" she said as she hurried over to the toilet block.

Alex felt sure Lee would not say anything about what had happened.

If ever Alex needed to have proof that he was not alone, he had been given a double helping today.

Now he found himself naturally walking with his head up and shoulders back as he went over to his favourite oak tree on the grassy bank. He touched the trunk before sitting on the grass and gently leant against it as he ate his lunch.

A short while later, he saw Lee, accompanied by the dinner lady, disappear inside the school building. Alex considered everything that had happened with Lee that morning. It was hard to believe. He wondered what would happen next.

When the bell went, Alex walked confidently towards the entrance of the school building. Yet again, there were Harvey and his mates loitering by the door.

They looked at Alex as he made his way over. He looked different. He was not walking with his shoulders drooping, head down and eyes focused on the ground as usual. They copied the way he was walking now, but exaggerated it by puffing their chests out and lifting their noses high in the air, making fun of him. Alex did not care. He just carried on walking through the door.

They soon started their old trick of pushing him, but Alex stopped, turned round to face them and smiled. At first they were surprised by his reaction, but then they got annoyed and they started to push him harder, until he lost his balance and fell over, landing on his knees. They hurt a lot from the previous fall, but Alex picked himself up and faced them again, still smiling. They pushed him over once more. This time he went sprawling and banged his elbow on the wall. He got up and turned slowly, still smiling. They were so frustrated that they could not upset him; they walked off, muttering angrily.

When they were out of sight, Alex sighed heavily. His whole body sagged with the effort he had made. He limped to his classroom. He felt as if he had won a small victory, even though they had hurt him again. In a small way, facing them had made him feel stronger, because he had not been completely cowed.

Alex checked his timetable. He had Latin with Mr Winter. He really enjoyed Latin, even though a lot of the children in his class thought it was a dead and useless language. Alex did not agree with this because it helped him to understand the origins of a lot of English words.

He made his way over to the language block. Today, they had to read the story of 'Daedalus and Icarus' in Latin and then translate it into English. Alex made short work of this and when they were asked questions about what had happened in the story, he was ready with his answers. It was fun.

At the end of the day, he had French which he did not like as much, as it was conversation. He found the accent hard.

After school, Alex rushed out of the gates and down the hill as quickly as he could.

As he approached his house, he saw Marguerite and Poppy in their beautiful front gardens. He waved to them both.

"How was your day?" Poppy asked.

"It's certainly been very eventful!" He grinned at her. "Thank you for your help."

"I am pleased that things worked out well," said Marguerite.

He went indoors and made a real fuss of the dog, calling her a 'daft hound' as she tried to catch his hands and rolled over to have her belly tickled. They careered up the stairs to deposit his satchel in his room and then rushed back down to go out for their walk. Alex felt he really needed some space. It had been an absolutely amazing day.

As they walked along, side by side, Alex talked to Willow about what had happened with Lee earlier in the day and how he might have got Harvey and his mates to register what they were doing to him. He told her how upset he was by what happened in art.

"Overall," he shared, "things don't seem to have become any easier, but somehow, I do feel a bit stronger."

Willow looked up at him with that earnest expression. She was always such a great listener!

When they reached Greenleah Heights, Alex took off her lead and she ran round and round in slowly decreasing circles until she stood panting in front of him. He threw her new tennis ball as far as he could – once, twice, three times. She kept retrieving it. Eventually she had had enough and lay down at his feet with her tongue lolling out of her mouth looking up expectantly at him.

Alex rewarded her with a treat and then they walked quietly along the path. Willow went off to sniff whenever she caught an exciting scent. She stopped to nibble blades of grass and came back looking quite comical with a long stalk hanging out of her mouth. She made Alex laugh.

Once they reached the top of the hill, they raced each other back down again. Alex thought it was fabulous to just run and run and not think about anything, to feel his muscles and lungs working and his blood pumping.

They both settled down in their comfy places in Alex's room when they got back home. Willow curled up at the bottom of the bed for forty winks. Alex picked up his new book about insects again. He really wanted to know more about beetles since he had seen that apparition. He went through the chapter several times looking closely at the diagrams and photos. There was one of those acetate sheets he could lift up to reveal the inside of the beetle too. It was fascinating.

It was soon time for Willow to have her dinner and for him to lay the table.

As the rest of the family filtered in, Alex's mum started dishing up. Tonight, it was sausages, mashed potatoes and peas. It tasted okay even though the sausages were rubbery, the mashed potato was lumpy, as usual and the peas were like bullets. No one complained though, and the food disappeared quickly as they ate, rather than talked.

Once Alex had helped his mum to clear away, he fetched his Latin homework. He had to learn a list of ten Latin words with their English meanings for a test at the end of the week.

In less than half an hour, he had them off pat and went into the front room to watch the end of a documentary. After it had finished, Scott raced off first, leaving Alex and Willow to trail after him.

Alex flicked through his insect book in his room while he waited patiently for his turn in the bathroom.

He was so engrossed in his book that his leg had gone to sleep. Willow was snuffling gently.

He wondered why Scott was taking so long. Perhaps he was reading one of his comics while sitting on the toilet. He did that sometimes. Alex waited a while longer, but when there was still no sound from the bathroom, he went to investigate.

"Get a move on, Scott!" he shouted.

There was no response.

The door was very slightly ajar so he pushed it a bit and called out again. "Are you okay?"

There was a muffled reply.

The door would not open fully as there was something stopping it on the other side.

Calling out again, "Scott, are you alright?" Alex put his shoulder to the door and pushed hard.

It opened enough for him to see Scott's feet sticking out from under what appeared to be a mountain of laundry.

Alex squeezed into the little gap in the doorway and braced himself against the door frame to push harder and managed to get through into the bathroom. He could hear that distinctive humming which told him that the angels were at work.

He began to pull at the clothing. There was a pair of trousers. He pulled and pulled and realised that they were Scott's, but giant sized. What on earth was happening here? Then he pushed an enormous jumper off the top and Scott began to scramble up through his gigantic shirt. The heavy, damp towel was still wrapped around his shoulders like a cloak as he tried to stand. Alex dragged it off him.

Scott sat down heavily on the toilet. He was visibly shaken and nearly as white as his crumpled shirt. His teeth were chattering so much that it was too difficult for Alex to understand what he was saying. Eventually, he was able to describe the saga.

"I'd just finished my wash, changed into my pyjamas and brushed my teeth. I was about to leave the bathroom when, suddenly, I was trapped underneath this lot! It was as if it had been dumped on me from the ceiling. It was so heavy and smelled so stale and fusty. I thought I was going to suffocate. It was as if I was in some crazy, mixed up dream."

Then he began to tremble again and his eyes were wide with fear as he peered around Alex. Alex turned his head and saw that the huge pile of laundry had disappeared and only Scott's normal sized clothes lay on the floor with his damp towel. Scott got up unsteadily.

"This is too weird! I need to get out of here!" he quavered.

He began to step over the mess on the floor. Alex realised what was going to happen and reached his hand out to stop him, but Scott pushed past.

As soon as he took a step out of the door, the dirty laundry began to get bigger and bigger, threatening to engulf him again.

In a panic, he rushed down the stairs, out of the back door and into the garden with the clothes and towel flapping behind him.

Alex ran after him and Willow flew down the stairs too. She snapped and growled at the clothes. Scott dashed about the lawn trying to avoid being trapped again, but he tripped and fell. He was soon covered by the heap again.

Alex desperately heaved the enormous, yellow jumper off him, with Willow pulling for all she was worth at the corner of the towel. He struggled with the weight and size of the clothing and could hear sobs issuing from the middle of the mound, when it began to shrink back to normal size.

Once he was free, Scott just lay there on the lawn, in the patch of light shining from the kitchen. He was curled into a ball, sobbing with his clothes lying around him

"Why's my stuff attacking me? What's going on? Make it stop. Please make it stop," he pleaded.

As he knelt beside Scott, Alex could see Marguerite peering over her fence and Poppy in an upstairs room at her house, observing the unusual scene on the lawn. They both looked sad and concerned.

Alex gave Scott a cuddle and helped him up off the grass. He held on to him as they began to make their way back into the house.

Scott kept looking over his shoulder fearfully, but his clothes and towel were just in an untidy heap on the lawn with Willow sitting on top of them. Then he caught site of Marguerite in the light from the back door and hung his head in embarrassment.

"I heard the commotion," she said. "I want to help you understand what is going on. I can see that this is all your stuff on the lawn and you know, as well as I do, that really it should be either hanging up or in the dirty washing basket."

Scott stared at her and then at Alex as if to ask what it was to do with her.

Alex quietly advised Scott, "Listen to Marguerite as she could help stop what is going on."

Scott thought he could see the arm of his shirt waving. He grabbed hold of Alex and looked pleadingly at Marguerite.

"I guess you always leave your stuff on the floor. I wonder if you do that just to upset Alex, who likes to have everything in its correct place," she continued.

Scott felt a little bit guilty, but he resented being in the spotlight and started to feel angry.

She carried on, "It is a disrespectful and lazy thing to do. You should clear up after yourself." She added, "If you are going to dump on Alex, you will get dumped on yourself!"

Scott was dumbfounded. He had never even met this woman before. He definitely was not expecting to be lectured on his behaviour by a complete stranger. He found his voice.

"Mind your own business," he said rudely.

He pulled away from Alex and marched towards the back door. However, his nightmare was not over. Through the open door, all sorts of items hurled themselves at him out of the air. A tee-shirt he had taken from Alex, pens, postcards and some old coins.

Alex caught a book as it sailed past him. He cried out in amazement. "Hey, this is my stuff that went missing from my room!" He tried to gather them up, but they kept flying at Scott who was trying to protect himself with his arms around his head.

"Stop it! Oh, please make it stop!" Scott pleaded. He sounded really frightened.

Marguerite called something over the fence. The hail of items stopped and everything made a pile at Alex's feet.

"I can see that all these items belong to Alex," she commented. "Do you realise that rummaging through Alex's stuff and taking his belongings, without his permission is wrong and causes Alex great upset?"

It was all getting too much for Scott. He was frightened and angry.

He yelled at Marguerite, "Why don't you butt out?" and lurched back into the house.

Alex went after him, wondering what would happen next.

Marguerite's voice followed them. "Scott, you need to understand that your actions will have consequences."

Scott hesitated before climbing the stairs. The television was loud and Harvey and their parents were all laughing at 'The Benny Hill show'. Alex wondered for a moment if Scott was going to tell them what had happened. If he did think this, he obviously changed his mind.

Back on the landing, they could both see the heap of enormous clothes spilling across the bathroom floor again. Outside Alex's room was a neat stack of all his stuff that had been 'borrowed'. On the floor outside Scott's room, were two of his favourite football posters. He rushed to pick them up, but they wafted tantalisingly just out of his reach.

"Scott, even if you don't like it," Alex tried to explain, "Marguerite has a point. You know how upset I get when you leave everything strewn on the floor for me to deal with and you also know how it makes me feel when my things are taken or moved without you asking."

At first, Scott seemed not to be listening. He just kept trying to retrieve his posters, but he grew tired. He sat down heavily on the top step and cried with frustration. Alex sat next to him and put his arm around his shoulders. They sat in silence together as the sound of laughter drifted up the stairs from the front room.

Scott eyed the elusive posters and craned his neck to look back into the bathroom where his normal sized clothes and damp towel still littered the floor. He realised that the mountain of stuff had been just those items he had worn in the day.

He guessed that somehow they had grown to huge proportions, maybe to measure out the number of times he had left them for Alex to clear away.

He felt dreadful as it dawned on him how thoughtless he had been in assuming that, as Alex liked things tidy, he would sort out the stuff left on the floor. He also remembered what a state Alex got in when he found his things had been tampered with.

With tears still glistening on his cheeks, he turned to Alex and said, "I'm sorry Alex, I didn't stop to think."

He was completely dejected and shuffled into the bathroom to collect his clothes. He put his uniform over the banister, the dirty things in the washing basket and then returned to hang his towel on the hook. He did not even look up at his posters still hovering near the ceiling. He opened his door and then turned again to Alex.

"I'm truly sorry. I promise that I'll never touch your stuff without asking and I'll always clear my things away when I've finished in the bathroom."

"Well, you've done a good job clearing away tonight," Alex told him. "Just remember that I'm quite happy to lend you things if you ask, as long as you promise to return them when you've finished or if I need them back."

Alex reached out and gave Scott a pat on his back as he crept into his room. He watched as the posters slipped through the closing door to their places on the wall.

For the first time in ages, they called out 'goodnight' to each other. Alex wondered how much his brother would remember of the night's events.

Alex quickly got ready for bed and snuggled up close to Willow. His mind raced with all that had happened that day. It had, without a shadow of a doubt, been the most unusual day of his life so far.

Eventually, he drifted off to sleep and soon found himself back in the beautiful garden. It was so sunny and hot there, he decided to lie down on the grass beneath the branches of an old oak tree for a while. As he lay there, he closed his eyes and listened to a bird singing nearby. It was idyllic.

Chapter 18

Alex woke to the sound of his mum yelling, "Rise and shine!"

Reluctantly, he got up, made his bed and waited for his chance to get into the bathroom. He was last today.

When he went into the kitchen with Willow, his brothers were already at the table. Scott looked a bit sore around the eyes as he looked up.

"You okay? Sleep alright?" he asked Alex.

Their mum turned and looked at Scott with a raised eyebrow. She probably wondered where this was leading, but Scott was not being sarcastic, just pleasant. Alex was pleased.

"Yeah, I'm okay. In fact, I slept like a log. How about you?"

Scott smiled knowingly at him and said, "I was a bit restless."

Harvey looked from one to the other at this unusual bit of conversation. "Scott must've had a bad dream or something in the night because he kept shouting at something to get off him while wrestling with his blankets," he added with a smirk.

Alex and Scott exchanged another knowing look. Harvey noticed this and felt left out of the secret they seemed to share. Usually Scott did not pay much attention to Alex. It seemed a bit odd.

Alex continued with his morning routine for Willow and then tucked into the bowl of runny porridge put out for him. He had a feeling that it was going to be another good, but different day.

The three brothers grabbed their bags and said their goodbyes before they left the house. As they walked to school, Scott kept dropping back as he tried to include Alex in their conversation that morning. Harvey got annoyed and physically tried to get between them.

Alex was surprised at suddenly being drawn in and, at first, it was all rather stilted. They chatted a bit about football, but Harvey kept trying to cut Alex out by talking over him to the point of shouting.

Scott changed the topic to what had happened to Lee.

Alex found it hard not to show his inside knowledge. He agreed with Scott that it was all rather strange and that it was not like Lee to be frightened of anything.

Harvey then got between his brothers and shoved them apart. Alex stumbled off the kerb and Scott staggered back. Scott got angry with Harvey.

"What's wrong with you this morning? Why're you behaving like such an idiot?"

Harvey began repeatedly shoving Scott in the chest. "You're the idiot! What's got into you today?"

"Leave off Harvey!" Scott said crossly.

"Stop it, both of you," Alex pleaded. He had never seen his brothers fight like this and somehow he felt that it was his fault. He was getting really distressed.

None of them had noticed Marguerite and Poppy backed up against the fence with their shopping bags clutched to their chests, trying to get out of the way.

Poppy put her fingers in her mouth and whistled sharply.

At the same time, Marguerite shouted, "Stop it at once!"

Scott and Harvey were so surprised, they did stop.

"Why on earth are you arguing and fighting in the street?" Marguerite was appalled.

"We're sorry," Scott said.

"Are you alright?" Alex asked worriedly.

However, Harvey was quite rude to them. "You should've moved out of the way. Anyway, it's nothing to do with you, you nosy cow!"

"Shut up, Harvey!" Scott was embarrassed. "I'm so sorry." He apologised again to the two women.

"Harvey, I am shocked to see how you treat your younger brothers. You should be the one to look after them."

Harvey shrugged and walked off.

"I hope you will stop being such a bully, especially to Alex at school!" Marguerite called after him.

This hit a nerve in Harvey and he turned back with real anger in his eyes. "You don't know anything! What's it to you anyway? You don't have any right to talk to me. You're not my parents."

"You need to mend your ways, and sharpish. Your actions will have consequences," Poppy added.

He laughed and pretended to quake with fear and then ran off.

Harvey's mood did not improve when he reached the playground and was unable to see Jimmy or Tommy anywhere. He waited near the entrance for them for a while.

Scott chose to stay with Alex. "I'm a bit worried about Harvey. He seems to have lost the plot. I don't understand what's going on for him. Why should he just turn on us like that?" Scott asked.

"I don't know," said Alex honestly. "I was scared by the way he was to you. You two are usually such good mates. I've never seen him be rude to adults either."

Alex was pleased to have some company after what had happened and was glad that he would have some time to recover. It was not the start to the day he had hoped for.

Scott turned the conversation to the events of the previous night. He wanted some explanations. "To be honest," he said, "it's a bit of a blur. It all happened so quickly. I know I was terrified. Wasn't it weird that Marguerite appeared in her garden? It was all a bit spooky." He carried on thoughtfully, "It was horrible being dumped on and all that stuff flying through the air." He shuddered. "I certainly don't want to go through that again!"

"I don't really know the ins and outs of it all, but I think that all will be well if you take responsibility for putting your stuff away and if you ask to borrow things from me instead of taking them whenever you feel like it," Alex said cautiously. The new friendship that was budding between them seemed very fragile and he did not want it to fall to pieces.

"I've certainly learnt a lesson and I'm really sorry for being so thoughtless and selfish. I'll definitely do better from now on," Scott told Alex.

Alex grinned at his younger brother and shook his long jumper sleeves like a ghost. Scott pretended to be scared and hid his head behind his arms. They both burst out laughing.

They chatted on about things they both liked, beside football. They found that they shared a keen interest in science and nature.

"You know," Scott told Alex, "you're really lucky to have such a choice of books in your room. I've got to admit that I'm a little envious of you as you always seem so knowledgeable. I think that Mum and Dad just see me as sporty and don't encourage me with books the way they do with you. I wish I had some books of my own."

"You can always ask to borrow my books," Alex offered. For the first time, he felt a connection with his younger brother. It gave him a lovely, warm feeling. They grinned at each other again.

Jimmy only lived three doors along from Tommy. He always knocked for him and they walked to school together. Luckily for him, Tommy was still at home as he was running late too. Jimmy waited on the doorstep while Tommy hurriedly put on his jumper and shoes. Then they both set off for school, sharing the bit of toast Tommy had quickly grabbed as he rushed past the kitchen.

When they came to the end of their road and turned the corner at the bottom of the hill, Marguerite and Poppy were standing at their front gates with their shopping. As the boys approached, Marguerite called them over by their names. They were surprised and, out of curiosity, they went over.

"Tell me boys, do you feel good when you join Harvey to bully and hurt Alex at school?"

This bald question shocked them.

"I have seen you pushing Alex around in the corridor every chance you get."

They gawped at her. How could she possibly have seen them? For a brief moment, an expression of guilt crossed their faces as they thought about what they had been doing to Alex. Then, because they felt exposed, they buried that feeling and replaced it with their usual nonchalant attitude.

"We don't know what you're talking about," Tommy asserted.

Marguerite had noticed their change of expression. "You boys really need to start thinking for yourselves. I believe you do know the right way to behave towards others, but you allow yourselves to be led astray. If you do not change your ways for the better, you just may have a taste of your own medicine."

"You need to think carefully about your actions because if you make the wrong choices, there will be painful consequences," Poppy added.

The boys felt uncomfortable and embarrassed. They became defensive. "Harvey is much worse than we are. You need to talk to him," Jimmy said. They turned their backs on the two women and ran off before anymore could be said. As they ran, they caught each other's eye and began to laugh.

Jimmy suddenly slowed to a walk and began to limp.

"My feet are really painful," he complained.

"You probably need a new pair of shoes. You wear them out so quickly playing football after school in them," Tommy suggested.

By the time they arrived on the school playground, Jimmy was desperate to sit down to take the weight off his feet. He found an empty bench and sat down while Tommy went off to find Harvey.

Jimmy took his shoes and socks off and sighed with relief. His feet had been so squashed. The end of his toes and the sides of his feet were red and sore so he gave them a gentle rub before attempting to put his socks and shoes back on.

Strangely, his socks were too small so he stuffed them in his pocket. He tried his shoes, but they were too small as well. He undid the laces and then tried again. Still they would not fit. He could not understand how his shoes and socks could have shrunk on the way to school. He had no choice but to keep them off so he put them in his bag for now. He hoped his feet felt normal by the time he was due to play football after school. They would probably be okay in his football boots he thought.

Barefooted, he trod gingerly over to his friends. They were deep in conversation. Harvey was having a moan.

"Scott's such a traitor! Suddenly he's started being all friendly to Alex and ignoring me," he told Tommy. "We had a bit of a set to on the way to school because he just made me so mad. Then I got told off by our neighbours who were on their way home from the shop."

"Yeah, well, those two busybodies caught me and Jimmy on the way to school and lectured us about how we treat Alex. They were trying to make us feel guilty," said Tommy. He chuckled, "You know what we should do. We should make sure Alex gets the message that we will not leave him alone just because he told on us to those old women."

Harvey nodded in agreement, even though he knew that Alex would not have said a word to a couple of strangers, as he had said nothing to his teachers or parents in the past. Things were beginning to sink in and tell him that maybe he needed to think about how he was behaving. That thought, however, did not take root. He caught sight of Jimmy limping towards them without his shoes and socks on. He pointed and started to laugh. Tommy joined in.

Jimmy tried to explain about his painful feet, but they were too busy making fun of him to listen to what he had to say. They had never, ever made fun of each other before.

Jimmy looked upset, so Tommy reached out to touch his shoulder. He wanted to reassure him that they were not being horrible. However, he ended up shoving Jimmy and jarring his own arm.

Tommy pulled his hand back and Jimmy stared at it. "You need to get your nails cut," he said.

That did not make any sense to Tommy because his nails were bitten down to the quick. He put his hands out in front of him and examined them. They did not look like his. All his nails were now long and sharp. He stared at them in disbelief, trying to figure out how this had happened. He gestured for Harvey and Jimmy to look at them.

"I already know you have long nails as they just dug into my shoulder," Jimmy said sarcastically.

"When did you decide to grow them?" Harvey asked. He then pranced around with one hand on his hip and the other at an odd angle, making fun of him.

"Listen, it's not funny you know," Tommy said. "Think about it. They couldn't have grown this long overnight. In fact, they were not like this when I left home. Something very weird is happening. I don't like it." Then he bit one of his nails off. No sooner had it been bitten off, it grew back again.

Jimmy laughed nervously as just then, his feet started to throb. He looked down at them. Tommy followed his gaze. He was sure they looked a little longer. To Jimmy they were beginning to feel like a small pair of flippers. They looked at each other in horror as they registered that something strange and entirely out of their control was happening to them. Harvey again felt left out.

The bell went and everyone made their way over to the school. Alex walked with Scott. 'The Terrible Threesome' was waiting by the door as usual but Jimmy and Tommy seemed distracted and upset.

Harvey glared at Alex and Scott. He pushed in between them and gave Alex an almighty shove which sent him sprawling full length in the corridor, banging his chin hard on the floor.

Scott was really shocked. He had never seen Harvey so aggressive to Alex, and at school. He rushed forward to help Alex who was holding his chin. There was a thin trickle of blood seeping out between his fingers.

Scott turned and shouted at Harvey, "What on earth are you playing at?"

He gave Alex a hand up and produced a relatively clean handkerchief to hold on his cut. He walked along, supporting him while he harangued Harvey.

"I can't believe you! You pick a fight with me on the way to school and you shove Alex into the road. You were so rude to the neighbours and now look what you've done! He's your brother and you've given him a bad cut on his chin. What's wrong with you?"

Harvey was gobsmacked by Scott rounding on him and had nothing to say.

Scott saw Alex to his desk and made sure he was okay before he rushed to his own class.

Several children had turned around and were now staring at Alex.

One girl went over to him. "You okay?" she asked.

"Yes, thank you," he mumbled. "I just fell down and hurt my chin, but I'm fine."

To distract himself from the attention of his classmates and the feelings swirling inside him, Alex reached for his notebook and pen and busily started writing.

It really upset him that Harvey had turned on Scott as well. It was all getting a bit much and he did not know what to do. Then he heard a faint humming which reminded him of the angels. He thought they must have a plan, but he wished he knew what it was. He tried to focus on his writing as he knew this would help him to calm down and face the day.

Harvey had never experienced Scott standing up to him in the way he had done this morning. He was shaken by this dramatic change. He looked for support from his friends, but they had gone on ahead, preoccupied with their own problems.

Jimmy was high stepping really awkwardly, trying to manage his flipper-like feet. Tommy was trying to hide his ludicrously, long nails under his armpits.

Harvey stood there feeling abandoned and alone.

Chapter 19

Wham! Out of the blue, Harvey was given an almighty shove on the back. He was completely taken by surprise and jerked forward. He was unable to keep his balance and landed awkwardly on his knees. He jumped up and swung around, but there was no one there. Mystified and a little shaken, he bent to rub his sore knees.

Bam! He was pushed on the bottom and before he could get his hands out to stop him, he staggered forward and cracked his head on the wall. He hardly dared to look around. He stood still and examined his head tenderly with his fingers. There was a bit of a cut, but it was not bleeding much.

He steadied himself by holding on to the wall. He twisted his head around, but again the corridor was empty. He was sure he could hear someone laughing at him. He hurried along to his classroom looking over his shoulder several times.

As he opened the door, something tripped him up. He staggered in and half fell on the girl sitting nearest the door. She let out a scream and pushed

Harvey off her. He banged into the next desk and the books and pens scattered onto the floor. He just could not get his balance and ended up measuring his length on the floor between the desks. The children were laughing and whispering and then there was silence. A pair of shiny, brown shoes appeared by his nose.

He pushed himself up onto his knees and focussed on the corduroy trousers in front of him. He then heard a quiet and menacing voice.

"Get up, if you please, Mr Angel." The teacher, Mr Robinson, was not impressed with his late and dramatic entrance. "Go to your seat." Mr Robinson wondered what Harvey was playing at.

"Sorry Sir," Harvey mumbled. "My brother fell over and cut his chin, so I was helping him and that made me late." He could not say that he had been pushed and tripped by an unseen assailant so he said, "I was in a hurry and had tripped over my own feet. Sorry for being late and for the disturbance." He seemed genuinely contrite.

Mr Robinson just said, "Get yourself sorted out. My lesson has been delayed long enough."

Harvey hid his bright red face as he bent to rummage in his bag.

The register had already been taken and Mr Robinson had just started handing out a textbook and a set of questions to everyone.

Harvey felt quite shaken by the turn of events in the corridor. He opened his book and began to read the passage set for comprehension. He could not concentrate. He did not look around at his friends. In any case, he felt that somehow they had betrayed him too. Everything seemed to be going wrong.

First, Scott had turned against him and then his friends had not supported him. There was that weird stuff in the corridor as if he was being pursued by a poltergeist or something freaky from a film. He turned to look back at the door in case whatever was following him had put in an appearance. There was nothing there. He shook his head and began reading the passage again.

Meanwhile, Jimmy was so relieved to be sitting down; he had not even opened his textbook. He popped his shoes and socks under his desk and stretched out his legs and wiggled his feet, letting out a long sigh just as Mr Robinson came up behind him. He looked disapprovingly at Jimmy's feet which were sticking out beyond his desk.

"Well young man, do you think you are still on holiday at the seaside?" he asked.

"No Sir, it's just that my feet are really painful and my shoes and socks don't seem to fit me anymore," he tried to explain.

Mr Robinson could see nothing mismatched between the feet and shoes he stared at, so he thought Jimmy was pulling a fast one.

"Put your shoes and socks back on this instant," the teacher ordered sternly. He waited.

Jimmy felt sure that he would be vindicated once Mr Robinson saw that his shoes and socks did not fit him. All eyes were on him. Jimmy pulled one sock on, and it fitted perfectly. Children began to laugh.

Mr Robinson glared around the classroom and then fixed Jimmy with a stare.

"Get the rest on, keep them on and stop making a fuss. I want no further disruptions in this lesson."

Jimmy was puzzled and so embarrassed.

By the time the teacher had finished handing everything out and had returned to the front of the class, Jimmy's feet started to feel very cramped and painful again. He tried his best to ignore this, but it became unbearable.

Once the teacher had signalled for everyone to start answering the questions on the sheet, as discreetly as he could, Jimmy removed his shoes and socks again, checking around him to make sure no one was watching him.

As he looked around, he noticed that everyone, except for Tommy had their heads down and were concentrating on their work. Tommy, however, seemed to be struggling with his pen, which fell with a clatter to the floor.

With his feet finally free again, Jimmy made a start on the questions in front of him. He was so focussed on his work that he did not hear the teacher moving quietly around the classroom, until he was tapped on the shoulder.

Mr Robinson pointed at his feet and scowled at him. Jimmy stuffed his feet back into his shoes as quickly as he could. Sure enough, they fitted perfectly again. The teacher indicated that he would be keeping his eye on him.

Jimmy tried to keep his attention on the questions and ignore the pain of his feet being squeezed and squashed, but he could not stand it anymore and took them off again.

"If you are going to continue to mess around and behave as if you are in holiday mode, then you will have an extra set of questions to do in detention after school!" Mr Robinson thundered.

"It's not my fault Sir, something's really happened to my feet!" Jimmy argued.

This angered the teacher so he gave Jimmy a detention and directed him to get on with his work. Jimmy was annoyed that he would not be able to play football after school. At least the teacher had not made him put his socks and shoes on again so he could spend the rest of the lesson in comfort. This was a very small consolation.

Once he had completed the work, he thought about what had happened to him. He hated being out of control and felt that Mr Robinson had treated him unfairly. Jimmy knew he would be the butt of everyone's jokes later. It was all so confusing and a bit scary.

On the other side of Harvey, Tommy was still struggling with his pen. The extra-long nails which had suddenly appeared were getting in the way. He just could not find a way to hold the pen so that he could write properly. His handwriting had not been good at the best of times, but now it was all over the place and even he had a job to read it. He tried gripping the pen higher up its shaft; he tried holding it in a fist; he tried placing the pen between different fingers and changing the angle, but still he could not write clearly. After about fifteen minutes of being unable to do any tidy work, Tommy gave up, put his pen down, folded his arms and sat quietly with tears of frustration coursing down his cheeks.

Mr Robinson glanced around the classroom and was surprised to see Tommy already finished, so he got up to have a look. He saw that most of the page was blank and the rest was covered in spidery writing so feint it could not be read.

"I'm really sorry Sir," Tommy told the teacher. "I can't use my pen properly because my nails are too long."

He promptly presented his hands for inspection. However, in the moment it took to untuck his hands, his nails had gone back to their normal, bitten, length. Both Mr Robinson and Tommy stared at them in disbelief.

Tommy's tears began to flow again. He did not understand what was happening to him.

The teacher thought Tommy was playing tricks to get out of work and to be funny. After the other two, he had had enough.

"Switch off the waterworks and get on with answering the questions. Otherwise you can do them in detention after school as well."

Tommy really did not want miss football after school. He and Jimmy were in the team.

He kept trying to get on with his work, but his nails had grown very long again. He managed a few more answers, but no one would be able to read what he had written. It was no use. He would have to accept that he was going to miss football.

As the teacher approached to check on him again, Tommy kept writing. He hoped that Mr Robinson could see that there really was a problem, but as soon as he got to Tommy's desk, his nails went back to normal. Tommy was bitterly disappointed that the teacher could not see what was going on and that the situation really was out of his control.

Jimmy and Tommy desperately tried not to draw attention to themselves for the rest of the morning, but they both gained another detention. They really began to feel that they were being singled out through no fault of their own and they did not like it one bit.

At lunchtime, they put their heads together and commiserated with each other. No one else could see what was happening and the teachers thought the boys were playing the fool for some obscure reason – maybe for a dare?

At first, the friends decided it was all Alex's fault and began plotting what they would do to him next. Then they realised how stupid this was as they agreed it was not possible that little Alex had any special powers. He did not even stand up for himself much. Eventually, they thought about how they had been to Alex. They recalled what the women had said to them that morning. They were not convinced that two old ladies could be doing this to them, but they were frightened.

It dawned on them that there must be some connection. They could not work it out exactly, but they were convinced it did have something to do with Alex and the two women. They were both still full of embarrassment, anger and frustration. They felt helpless as the thought of the afternoon lessons loomed.

Then it registered with them that this must be how Alex felt every time they did something rotten to him. They realised from the morning's experiences that it was no fun being out of control.

They had been warned this morning so they concluded that if they tried to be nicer to Alex, then maybe things would start to get better for them.

After the initial upset, Alex had a good morning. At lunchtime, he went and sat on the grassy bank under the oak tree, even though it was a little chilly. With his jumper sleeves protecting his hands from the cold, he ate his favourite packed lunch.

He thought about Scott and how he had seen a new side to him this morning. He had chosen to be caring and protective of him and had spoken up for him. Alex liked the feeling of having someone on his side. He was even more pleased when Scott came over to sit with him after he had finished his dinner in the hall.

"You know what happened this morning in the corridor?" Scott asked. "Was that a one off, or has it happened before?"

Alex felt he no longer had to hold it all in, so the whole truth of his nightmare with Harvey, Jimmy and Tommy came tumbling out. He also told his brother about Lee (but not all of it) and Mrs Bartlett, the new art teacher.

Scott looked really sad. "I had no idea how hard the last year and now the beginning of the new term has been for you," he said.

They sat quietly beside each other, lost in their own thoughts until the bell went, then they walked back together.

Tommy and Jimmy were near the door but, this time, they went inside first without even looking at Alex. With the relief of not having to endure further torment and the change in Scott, Alex almost floated down the corridor to his class.

Tommy quickly went to the toilet before registration. He wondered how he would manage with his long nails. As he went to undo the zip of his trousers, he let out a whoop. The talons had disappeared and he had his familiar, nail-bitten fingers back. He rushed out to find Jimmy.

Jimmy was sitting in the cloakroom with a silly grin on his face. He was looking at his feet, comfortably inside his socks and shoes.

He started to laugh and shouted out, "They fit! They fit!"

It had been painful, but they had learned their lesson. They would never be nasty to anyone again, no matter who tried to persuade them.

The afternoon passed quickly as they were kept on task. They had no time to think about the strange and frightening events of the day. Tommy and Jimmy were dreading detention.

Harvey was really looking forward to football practise until he remembered his mates would not be there. He felt rather gloomy as he got ready. The two reserves, who were chosen to replace Tommy and Jimmy, were older boys and did not seem very friendly.

During the warm up, one of them deliberately tripped Harvey up and sent him sprawling.

"Oi! What did you do that for?" Harvey shouted at them.

"Stop messing around over there and get on with it!" shouted the coach, glaring at Harvey.

As they ran around the pitch, the two boys ran either side of Harvey and kept crossing in front of him so that he had to pull up sharply. The boys behind piled into him. This happened several times and the coach called him out for disrupting the practise. Harvey was not used to this as he usually received praise. He sat on the bench fuming. It was not his fault.

At half time, he was swapped in. By then, he was cold and miserable. During the game, the two reserves played in such a way as to get Harvey told off for dangerous tackling and being offside. He hardly got to see the ball.

At the end of the game, the coach remonstrated with Harvey. "If you do not change your attitude, you will be off the team."

The two boys sniggered behind him.

Harvey felt horrible. Not only had he been picked on mercilessly by something in the corridor, these boys seemed to have it in for him for no reason. Jimmy and Tommy would be out for several practises yet, so Harvey felt really dejected. He wanted to get home and have a good moan to Scott. This had been the worst day ever.

Chapter 20

Alex set off home on his own at the end of the day. He heard someone shouting his name. It was a novel sensation to see Scott running towards him with a big grin on his face. He wanted to tell Alex all about the experiment they had done in his chemistry lesson.

"We did this experiment today to separate out colours in ink," he explained. "First, we had strips of special paper to hang off a little stick. One strip had a water soluble marker line at the bottom and the other, a permanent marker line. When we dipped them in a beaker of water, lots of different colours sort of grew up the paper like rainbow stripes. The darkest colour, purple, was at the bottom. The colours separated out and yellow travelled the furthest up the paper. It was fascinating to watch. The permanent marker one didn't change.

We were given beakers with a special kind of alcohol in it for the next experiment. Matt pretended that he was going to drink his and lifted it to his lips as a joke. The teacher gave him a real telling off and said that chemistry was not for messing around in.

We tried the experiment again, but there were no pretty colours, even though a blackish smudge moved a little bit up the paper. We had to do some boring calculations at the end and write up the experiment," Scott finished.

He then dug around in his bag and showed Alex the rainbow of colours that had come out of the ink. Alex was amazed, not only at the results of the experiment, but at the way Scott was so eager to share it with him.

Alex opened the front door to find an excited Willow. She was wagging her tail and jumping up at him. He made a real fuss of her.

"Hello, my lovely girl. It's so good to see you. Did you miss me? Did you? Did you? Well I missed you," he said.

Scott patted Willow too.

"You're lucky to have your own dog and she's so lovely," he said enviously.

"Yes, I know. She's my best friend," he acknowledged.

Alex ran off happily to get her ready for their walk up to Greenleah Heights while Scott disappeared upstairs.

Scott changed and lay on his bed thinking about what he had seen and heard that day and what to do about it. He made up his mind.

He jumped up and went to find his mum. She was in the kitchen and offered him a cup of tea as she had just boiled the kettle.

He had decided to speak up for Alex and wanted to do it before Harvey and his dad got home. They sat together at the kitchen table and Scott began to tell her about what he had seen Harvey do to Alex at school earlier. He also mentioned that Jimmy and Tommy had joined Harvey in bullying Alex over the last year.

When he had explained everything, he said, "I didn't know anything about it until today. Did you know?"

His mum was really shocked. "Alex has never said a word to us about any of it," she replied quietly. She looked so sad.

He knew how she must be feeling.

"You've done the right thing in telling me. I will sort things out with Harvey."

Scott was relieved to have told her, but was worried about how Harvey would respond when he found out. He decided to make himself scarce and went off to see if his friends would come out to play football before dinner.

The front door slammed, telling his mum that Harvey was home. Obviously, he was not in the best of moods. She called him into the kitchen.

"You want a cup of tea?" she offered. "Sit down."

He did as he was told, sensing that something was wrong as his mum looked very serious.

"Is there anything you need to tell me?" she asked.

He shook his head and looked at her with a puzzled expression.

She paused and studied his face. He began to feel uncomfortable.

"Tell me about what happened to Alex today," she requested.

"I accidentally bumped into him today in the corridor and he fell over and hurt himself," he blustered.

"I know you're lying to me," she stated. "You should think carefully about what you say next." Her tone held a subdued note of anger.

Harvey realised he was not going to be able to wriggle out of telling his mum the truth by sidestepping and putting the blame elsewhere, or by getting her off the point with a row. He also knew that sitting in silence would not put her off either, as she would keep on at him. He hated being nagged.

"Okay. So I pushed him over. He deserved it. He's started to muscle in on my friendship with Scott. He's got no right to come between us."

His mum was surprised by this response. She had no inkling of rivalry between the boys, but more importantly, she wondered how this could be seen as a legitimate excuse for what he had done. Her anger was tinged with sadness.

She pressed on. "How long has this been going on? Were you and your mates bullying Alex all last year?" she asked incredulously.

Harvey laughed. "Yes it's true," he stated. His face became hard and angry.

She could not believe this response. "How could you be so nasty to your own brother? For over a year as well! This is all so wrong. I don't know what to think. Being the older brother, you should have been protective of Alex."

Harvey just shrugged his shoulders.

Harvey's attitude made her blood boil. "Are you trying to show me that you just don't care? I hope you're not that hard. This has really shocked me. I had no idea of what has been going on, and for a whole year! Why? Harvey, Why?" she asked.

"We both need to think about what's gone on here. This is serious," she continued. "You're grounded for the next week, my son. No seeing friends, no football and no telly. Unless I see a change in attitude and in your behaviour towards Alex, you will be grounded for longer. I want you to show some respect for your brother and a lot more kindness. Now go up to your room and stay there until I call you down for dinner."

Harvey groaned. Hanging his head, he slouched out of the room.

His mother remained at the table, shaking with emotion, until the front door banged open and Alex and Willow bounded in.

Alex took off Willow's collar and lead and then washed his hands. He refilled the water bowl. His mum had said nothing so they left her to her cup of tea and quiet sit down. Halfway up the stairs, he heard his mum calling him back down.

In the kitchen, his mum was by the sink rinsing her cup out. She turned slowly, walked over to him and wrapped her arms around him.

"I love you. You're so special to me and your dad," she said as she kissed his head.

Alex did not know what had brought this on, but it felt nice.

"Sit with me for a bit. We need to have a chat," she said.

Alex sat down and waited. He had absolutely no idea what she wanted to talk to him about. He noticed that she looked a bit upset and wondered what had happened.

She took a deep breath. "Scott told me earlier what has been happening with Harvey and his friends at school."

At first, Alex's stomach churned. He had a mixture of feelings as he could not anticipate the outcome of his problems being out in the open. He worried about Harvey's reaction to Scott and to him. He wondered if his mum really believed Scott. He thought his dad might think he should have stood up for himself more. Maybe he should not have just turned the other cheek. His mum cut across his thoughts.

"I'm so glad that Scott saw what happened today and that you were able to tell him about what's been going on. A whole year, Alex, and you never came to me or your dad. Not once did I get a sense that there was any problem." She shook her head in disbelief. There were tears in her eyes. "Tell me what's been happening since you've been back at school. Is it just Harvey and his mates or is there anyone else?"

Alex began to talk. It was a relief to tell her about it all and how he had tried to cope. "The beginning of term was awful," he confessed. "Harvey, Tommy and Jimmy would not leave me alone when they met me in the corridor. They pushed and shoved me all the time and when I fell and hurt myself, they just laughed. No one helped me until Scott was there and saw what Harvey did. He was really mad at him."

The floodgates had opened and he let it all out. "There's another boy, called Lee. He punched and kicked me and pulled some of my hair out just because I was trying to stop him from being cruel to insects. He caught a daddy longlegs and pulled its legs off one by one. Then he squished a lovely butterfly, just to upset me. Yesterday, he caught a beetle." Alex shuddered at the memory, but he said nothing about the other strange events.

His mum stared at her gentle boy who could not bear to see cruelty.

"Is there anyone else being horrible to you?" she asked.

"Well," he said, "Mrs Bartlett made me sit at the front of the class. I was really upset and in tears for the whole lesson. She ignored me and didn't give me any help like she gave the others. I did try to explain how difficult it is to manage when I'm at the front, but she didn't seem interested."

"Why didn't you tell me or your dad about all this?"

"I didn't want to cause any upset, and besides I didn't expect anyone to listen or believe me."

"We want you to tell us whenever there's anything bothering you, no matter what. We love you dearly. We want what's best for you. We want you to be happy." She went on to say, "I feel so guilty and sorry that I wasn't able to protect you. I'm sorry if I haven't always listened to you in the past. I feel that I've really let you down." She got up and moved round behind him. She hugged him again and kissed the top of his head.

It was all getting a bit much for Alex so he wriggled out of her arms and off his chair.

"Its okay, Mum. I know you and Dad love me." He hastily put Willow's food down and escaped upstairs to get on with his homework.

Some of his anxieties had lifted. He was pleased that his family was beginning to understand him. He was not so much the odd one out any more. Now the truth was out, he hoped things would continue to improve.

He heard his dad come home and then raised voices in the kitchen. His dad sounded really angry and he could hear his mum trying to placate him. Eventually, it went quiet and his dad came up to wash and change. He knocked on Alex's door.

He sat on the end of the bed and put his hand on Alex's shoulder.

"I'm so sorry about what's been going on. I can't believe what Harvey's been doing. I know your mum is dealing with things, but I want you to know that you can always talk to me." He paused a while, then said, "I know I've told you in the past that you need to toughen up, but actually I'm really proud of your gentle nature." His voice was breaking. "Even if I'm tired and falling asleep in front of the telly, I still want to know what's going on for you, whether it's good or bad. I'll try to make sure we get a chance to talk away from the others from now on."

Alex did not know quite what to say so he just got up and gave his dad a hug. His dad patted his back several times before he disappeared into the bathroom.

Dinner that night was late and it was a rather strained affair. No one gave eye contact or chatted. Alex thought his dad looked tired and grim.

After dinner, Harvey went straight up to his room followed by his dad. Alex was excused from clearing up as his mum wanted some time on her own. He and Scott went into the front room. They could hear the sound of raised voices upstairs so they switched the television on and sat together awkwardly.

Alex broke the silence between them. "I'm glad that everything's out in the open. I hope Harvey doesn't start to be horrible to you now."

"I'm sure it will be okay. Harvey can be really fun you know," he replied.

Alex was not too sure about that, but then again, he was beginning to see a different side to Scott. They watched the programme together until their parents came in, then they both went off to their rooms.

Harvey was really angry that Scott had told his mum about what had been happening at school.

"I'm sorry Harvey, but I just couldn't let it carry on. I've never seen that side of you before and I was scared for Alex. I've seen you get mad with me or your mates, but it wasn't scary like that. It was like you changed into this hateful being."

Harvey said nothing, but sat on the edge of the bed, picking at the skin around his finger nails.

Scott continued, "I've been thinking. I can understand a bit how Alex must've felt when we cut him out all the time. I don't know why we did that because he's okay really, in an Alex sort of way. Okay, so he's a bit of a swat and he doesn't get jokes and stuff, but he's not that bad."

Scott trailed off as Harvey glowered at him across the room.

"Well, anyway," he continued, "I think we've not been fair. Just because it doesn't take much to upset him, doesn't mean we should. He's got feelings too and I think we should try to be nicer to him."

Harvey, now lying on his side with his back to Scott, let out a loud "Humph!"

Scott was not put off. He continued, without going into the details, "Some surreal stuff happened to me the other day, to do with how I never clear up after myself and take things from Alex without asking. It made me see that I was being really unkind and selfish."

Harvey sat up. "That stuff that happened to you, was it what you had the dream about?"

"Yeah, it was weird and scary."

Hearing this encouraged Harvey to share what had happened to him.

"You mustn't laugh," he warned. "Something attacked me in the corridor and pushed me over when I got into class." He looked at Scott. There was no sign of a snigger so he carried on. "Then, in football practise there were these two bigger boys who had it in for me and got me in trouble with the coach. It was the worst practice ever. I even thought that I might stop playing."

"Woah! You must have been feeling pretty fed up!" commented Scott.

"It was horrible. First that 'thing', then the boys and even the coach was picking on me for no good reason." Harvey shook himself as if to get rid of the memory or feelings. "It's been such a mixed up day," he continued. "Now I come to think about it, weird stuff was happening to Jimmy and Tommy too. Jimmy was saying about his feet growing or something and he couldn't keep his shoes and socks on. He got a detention off Mr Robinson. Tommy suddenly had these really long nails like a witch or something. He couldn't do his work and he got a detention too. That's why they weren't at football."

Everything seemed to have been against him. It was very confusing and seemed so unfair, especially as he was now grounded. Harvey was full of self-pity. He began to cry and stuck his head under his pillow. He was too old to react like this!

After a while, he was quiet and Scott thought he had fallen asleep. He began to read his comic but could not really concentrate. After he had read the same bit several times, he slapped it down on the bed beside him. Harvey rolled over.

"I suppose," he said cautiously, "thinking about it, whatever 'it' is that has been doing things to everyone, 'it' is making us feel a little bit of how Alex must feel a lot of the time."

Harvey sat up and peered at Scott. Scott looked very thoughtful and sad.

Harvey continued, "I know I've been horrible to Alex for ages. For some reason he seems to bring out the worst in me. I can't help it. He's just so annoying and it can be funny winding him up. I guess it all got out of hand when I encouraged Jimmy and Tommy to join in." Harvey stopped.

He suddenly realised that, what he had thought of as a joke, was actually bullying. He had not understood until today, when he was pushed around by 'the presence', or whatever it was, just how helpless and alone Alex must have felt. Harvey had hated those feelings himself and now felt really ashamed of what he had done to Alex for such a long time.

Things had been going around in Scott's mind too. "You know," he began, "we haven't been very good brothers to Alex. I know he's the one in the middle and he's very different from us, but we've either been mean to him, thoughtless or downright horrible. I, for one, feel really bad. He's a big brother to me, but I've never given him a chance.

Today, I was talking to him about chemistry and it was really nice as he was so interested, even though he probably did all that stuff last year. He's so into all that kind of thing, he probably knows loads which we could share in a nice way, if you know what I mean."

"You're right," agreed Harvey. "I feel really mean and stupid. After all, he can't help how he is and he's younger than me, so I should look out for him more. I just focus on the things that wind me up. I know he's a good kid really. Do you know what? I think he probably knows as much about football as I do. I just never give him a chance."

The brothers got themselves ready for bed and went to sleep wondering how they could make it up to Alex.

Alex had not been able to settle to reading. He was aware of Harvey and Scott's voices across the landing. Even though the television had been on, he could hear his parents talking too. He sat on his bed hugging Willow. All went quiet in his brothers' room. He heard his parents come upstairs.

He realised that he was really cold. He quickly got undressed and posted himself under the blankets. He tried to keep as much of his body on the warm bits from where he and Willow had been sitting. Even so, he was shivering and exhausted, but questions kept going round in his mind. Why was Harvey so mean? Was it his fault?

Eventually, all the emotions of the day caught up with him and he drifted into a fitful sleep.

Chapter 21

Once more, he was transported to the beautiful garden and found the angels waiting for him by a sparkling stream. It reminded him of the one near his gran's where he played with Patrick in the summer. They both looked sad.

"What's wrong?" Alex asked them.

Marguerite sighed and said, "Our time on Earth is running out." She explained, "When the flowers in our gardens have shed all their petals, it will be time for us to leave."

Alex was devastated. He had only just been reunited with these two wonderful beings. He could not believe that they would be leaving so soon.

"Your life will be much easier now that the wheels of change have been set in motion," said Poppy. "Your gift will become clearer to you and you will quickly learn how to use it, so we will no longer be needed here."

Alex pleaded with them to stay, but Marguerite said, "I wish we could stay too, but we have received instructions to return home."

The sense of loss was overwhelming and tears made little rivulets down his cheeks.

Marguerite gently cupped Alex's face in her hands. He looked into her beautiful, clear blue eyes.

"Don't be sad," she said. She went on to explain, "You will be able to see us still if you need our help or advice. You can visit us in this garden whenever you like."

Poppy reassured him, "We will be keeping our beady eyes on you!"

Alex smiled with relief.

They sat quietly together looking into the clear water as it rippled around the rocks. Alex thought this would be a good time to ask the question about Harvey that had been bothering him for as long as he could remember.

"Why is Harvey so set against me? It's like he really hates me? What can I do?"

Marguerite sighed and began to explain, "Jealousy has twisted the way Harvey thinks."

"What's Harvey got to be jealous about?" Alex asked.

"Before you were born, Harvey got all the attention," she continued. "When the new baby came along, Harvey felt left out. Then as you got older, he felt you did not need him because you had such a close and exclusive bond with Willow.

As you grew up, you were bright and seemed to do everything the right way. He felt he could not compete.

When Scott came along, he found an ally as they were similar in nature, so he gave up on you. He still carries the old resentment with him and, without being conscious of it, is afraid that you might take Scott away from him. That was why, when things began to change, his jealousy and resentment quickly turned to anger."

Alex could see things from Harvey's perspective a little, but thought it was a bit daft really. He wished Harvey had not given up on him. At least now he knew the reason for his behaviour.

Poppy then told Alex, "I know that Harvey is truly sorry for all the hurt he has caused you." She said, "He has had time to think about things seriously, and now he needs you to forgive him, before both of you can move on to being better brothers."

Alex wondered how that was going to happen. He hardly saw Harvey anyway and now he would be even more fed up with him as he had been found out, told off and grounded.

They began walking to an area of the garden he had not seen before. It was more formal and had beds of flowers not unlike the angels' earthly gardens. There were lots of benches dotted around.

Poppy made him laugh when she said, "I need to talk seriously to you about your ears."

Without thinking, he covered them with his hands.

She said, "We know that you have very sensitive hearing which has caused you a great deal of distress. I must say, you have done really well to find strategies which help you to keep calm and refocus." Then she asked him, "I wonder if you have been hearing new sounds or voices recently?"

Alex thought about it, even though it seemed an odd question.

"Think back to the day we met in the back garden," Marguerite suggested.

Alex remembered then. "Oh," he said, "you mean the humming sound and voices singing." Then he recalled that he had heard the humming when he felt as if someone was watching him and also when he saw Lee in the toilet block with the little beetle. He had just put that down to the bizarre things that had been happening.

Poppy explained, "You have the ability to hear things that no one else can. This is the special gift you were born with."

Alex was not sure he valued this gift greatly, as he could already hear too much for his liking. What she went on to say really surprised him and was very hard to understand.

"You have the ability to hear the inner voices of young people who need help of some sort or are sad, confused or angry."

At first, Alex felt that he had enough trouble dealing with the overt anger of people around him without having to cope with inner voices too. He wondered what he was expected to do, supposing that he could actually hear anything other than humming and voices singing.

Marguerite knew that it was very confusing for Alex so she tried to explain simply. "Your ears are like a radio receiver. Lots of voices from different people will travel to you and bounce around like the static and crackles of radio waves. Some will be clear for a moment and then fade away. Sometimes, you will be overwhelmed by a whole cacophony of voices vying for your attention. You will have to learn to tune in to the most important voice and how to switch off. Until you know how to control the flow of the voices, you will hear them all at once and they will sound loud and incoherent."

"When you need to switch the voices off, all you need to do is to use your own inner voice to ask for silence." Poppy continued, "In order to hear only one voice at a time, you should ask for one voice to come forward. You will learn to judge who needs to be heard and whom you can help. Your skills will develop and mature over time. We will be looking after you and guiding you, even when we are no longer actually here with you."

"Embrace and cherish your differences and gifts because they are the very things that make you the lovely, special person that you are," Marguerite advised.

He felt a little embarrassed, but chuffed at the same time because they seemed to think he was okay.

Marguerite said, "We will begin with a lesson now."

Alex was a little surprised and nervous.

"Look around," she said.

To his astonishment, there were lots of people now sitting on the benches, chatting. Children were playing on the grass and groups of teenagers were messing around under the trees.

Alex stared and, before he could help himself, wondered out loud, "Where have all these people come from?"

His eye was drawn to one elderly man who raised his hand in a familiar wave. It was Mr Andrew, his old neighbour! It was unsettling for Alex to think that he might be in Heaven, but not dead.

Poppy was quick to reassure him. "All these souls are here at the moment to help you with your first lesson. It will be a bit like drama class," she said encouragingly.

Alex froze. He hated drama, as he never understood what was going on and could not improvise.

Poppy put her arm around his shoulder and laughed.

"Don't worry," she said, "all you have to do is to listen. There is no acting required on your part! All these people will be taking on roles and will be trying to get through to you with their inner voices."

Alex felt quite daunted.

When Poppy gave a signal, he reeled backwards, clutching his head. The din was awful. Marguerite put her finger to her lips, reminding him to call for silence. He closed his eyes and clenched his fists as he tried to focus, but the overwhelming noise continued.

Still holding his ears, he looked to Poppy for help. She mimed closing her eyes, being still and breathing deeply. He tried to relax by counting his breaths in and out. He closed his eyes and thought of silence. There seemed to be fewer voices. Using his inner voice he asked for silence and the voices hushed.

He had done it. He opened his eyes and was about to tell the angels, but the voices began to build again. This time it was easier to focus and soon peace descended.

Marguerite then put her hand behind her ear to remind him that he had to concentrate on one voice.

He looked around the group and saw a young lad on his own, kicking angrily at the roots of a tree. Alex used his inner voice to ask that lad's voice to come forward. He heard him loud and clear. The lad told him that his dad had left home and that he hated his stepdad. Alex switched off again.

He sat on the nearest bench feeling at once elated and wiped out. When he looked around again, everyone had gone and Marguerite and Poppy were sitting either side of him.

"Well done Alex. You tried so hard and really managed to get some control. Not bad for a first go!" Marguerite praised him.

"You made a good choice from the actors and their scenarios," added Poppy.

Alex thought he would get the hang of switching on and off and even of making good choices, but wondered what he was expected to do then.

The angels left Alex so that he could get some rest.

Chapter 22

The following morning, the mood at breakfast was very different as Harvey had gone to school early. Scott and his mum chatted about how Jimmy and Tommy were in so much trouble for skiving and cheeking the teachers.

When Alex went into the kitchen, Scott turned to him and asked, "Will you help me with the science project I have to complete before half term?"

"Okay," Alex replied readily. "What's it about?"

"Dunno. I haven't decided yet."

Scott was really excited that Alex had agreed and Alex liked the feeling of being included.

After breakfast, Scott and his mum walked to school with Alex. Since she had found out about the bullying, she decided to see Mr Adams. She also wanted to make sure that all the staff knew that Alex was a hard worker and was no trouble at all. She wanted to discuss the need for understanding and support in the classroom for Alex. She knew that if they reduced his levels of distress, he would be able to cope better with his work and realise his potential in all his lessons.

Alex walked tall. He had reinforcements with him today and it felt good. At the school gate, Alex's mum kissed both him and Scott on their foreheads.

"Love you both. Have a good day."

Scott was embarrassed and looked around to make sure this had not been seen. Alex felt all warm and fuzzy.

Their mum rushed off to the reception area to find Mr Adams.

Alex and Scott sat together by the oak tree on the grassy bank, talking about possible ideas for the science project until it was time to go in.

At the school entrance, they spotted Jimmy and Tommy. Harvey was nowhere to be seen. Alex tensed in anticipation even though Scott was with him, but Jimmy and Tommy just smiled sheepishly at him.

Alex could hardly believe this turnaround and walked along happily behind them. He checked over his shoulder once in case Harvey put in an appearance though.

It had been a brilliant start to the day. Alex really enjoyed his morning and it seemed to fly by.

About half-an-hour before lunchtime, Mrs Anderson, one of the school's administrators, came into Alex's classroom and spoke quietly to Mr Dear.

Everyone was busy tidying their maths things away when Alex heard his name being called. He went up to the desk and gulped when he was told to go along to Mr Adams' office. Although he knew he had done nothing wrong, he felt as if he must be in trouble, maybe because of what his mum had told the headmaster.

Alex sat on the edge of one of the hard chairs outside Mr Adams' office and waited to be summoned.

Mrs Anderson showed him into the headmaster's office. Alex was invited to sit opposite Mr Adams with the huge desk between them.

"Now Alex," he began, "there is nothing to be worried about. You know that your mother came to see me this morning." He paused.

Alex nodded and waited for him to go on.

"I would like you to tell me yourself what has been going on because I would like to hear about it from your perspective."

Alex needed quite a bit of reassurance and prompting because he felt really uncomfortable talking about his brother and the other boys. Somehow, although he knew that what they were doing was wrong, he felt as if it was his fault. He thought that he should not be telling tales. On the other hand he knew that he had to get it sorted out because he was not able to cope anymore. He wanted it to stop so that he could enjoy the whole of his school day without worrying about who may happen to set upon him.

By the time he had finished what he had to say and had answered all Mr Adams' questions, he was drained.

"I shall be talking to the boys concerned and dealing with the whole issue of bullying in our school on a wider level. This kind of behaviour will not be tolerated. I am glad that you had the courage to speak up. I know it has been hard for you. In the future, I want you to speak up more quickly if anything happens and not leave things to get worse over a length of time. We will make sure that things are made easier for you in art as well." Mr Adams stood up to signal the end of the meeting. "I shall be informing your mother of the outcome later in the day. You had best get back to class now. Mrs Anderson will give you a note for your teacher." Mr Adams moved around the desk and opened the door.

Alex felt relieved that it was all over, but was worried how people would react to what Mr Adams said to them.

He got back to class and handed the note to the teacher. He was given some homework and sent off for lunch.

Alex collected his packed lunch from his locker and walked outside into the warmth of the autumn sun. He went over to the grassy bank, pressed his hand to the trunk of the oak tree, and then sat beneath its branches. He ate his lunch while looking around at the other children. As he scanned the playground, he noticed Lee sitting alone on one of the benches by the wall of the school building. He was hunched over and looking thoroughly dejected.

Alex felt a sudden wave of sadness. He sensed that he needed to try out his new listening skills. He knew from first-hand experience, that Lee was a very angry and hurt person who took out his feelings on other children and defenceless creatures. He did not like the way he behaved, but knew somehow that he had to hear what was going on for him.

Alex focussed on Lee and listened very carefully. At first, there was nothing but a confusion of voices. Alex remembered to ask for silence. He then singled out Lee's inner voice.

Lee was thinking about his older brother, Gary. That morning, he had shoved Lee's head into the washing up bowl full of dirty water. This was because Lee had said it was not fair he should always have to clear up in the kitchen. He had pointed out that he had to go to school and Gary was at home all day. He thought he was going to drown before he managed to wriggle out of his grasp.

Ever since he could remember, Gary had always bullied him to do things. He was big and strong and stank of beer. His head was shaved and he thought that he was really hard, especially when he went out with his gang of friends. He had a foul temper and used his fists on his mum too. Lee's dad was away most of the time working in the merchant navy.

Once, Gary held Lee upside down by his ankles over the banisters until he promised to clean his room for him and put his dirty clothes in the washing machine. Lee was only about seven at the time.

Now his mum was working more shifts at the factory, Lee was terrified of what would happen next. He did not feel that he could go to anyone for help as the last time he had tried, Gary found out and Lee ended up with a broken arm.

Because he was bullied at home, he felt helpless, frightened and angry. Sometimes, he would take these feelings out on children who annoyed him. Sometimes, he tormented insects he found, taking delight in their suffering.

Now the bugs had turned on him! He was not surprised. He did not really like the person he had become. In fact, nobody seemed to like him. He could not blame them. He thought his life might be a bit more bearable if only he had a friend he could trust.

As Alex listened, he looked at Lee and felt so sorry for him.

Lee suddenly realised that he was being stared at and his face turned angry. Alex held his gaze and gave him a friendly smile. Lee made a rude gesture and turned his back on him.

Alex was shocked by what he had heard and began to understand why Lee behaved the way he did. It was all he had known. Alex had felt something of the hurt and pain that Lee was in, as well as his sadness, desperation and loneliness. He remembered what the angels had said about Lee being his 'first assignment'.

He did not know what he would do or say, but he found himself going over to sit at the other end of the bench from Lee.

He plonked his satchel on the bench and it tipped over. Out fell his new book on insects. Alex picked it up.

"Would you like to have a look at it?" he asked, as he put it on the bench between them.

It fell open at the page about stag beetles. Lee stared at it and then at Alex. So many emotions crossed his face; it was hard to read what was going on for him. He said nothing.

Alex stretched out his legs and looked over towards the toilet block.

"That giant beetle was terrifying, wasn't it? Never seen anything like it! What happened was just so weird; I never said anything to anyone." Lee said nothing, so Alex continued, "What do you reckon it was all about?"

There was a long pause and then Lee said in a very subdued voice, "It was really scary, especially when the beetle had hold of my arm." Lee looked sideways at Alex as if to judge how much he should say. He confided, "It reminded me of my brother." He shuddered and seemed to get lost in his own thoughts again. "That beetle was certainly huge, strong and scary!" he commented.

They sat quietly, staring at the toilet block. Lee thought about it again and about Alex. They had a shared experience, where both of them had been victims in different ways. Alex had not told anyone. He was talking to him even though he had landed some punches on him. He seemed to understand. Lee was coming to the conclusion that this quiet kid might become a friend.

Lee suddenly turned to Alex and blurted out, "I'm sorry for the way I've treated you. I know I was wrong, but I was feeling so angry and mixed up, I just took it out on you." He went on to say, "After the giant beetle, I realised that it was not right to pick on you because you tried to save the insects. I did know deep down that I was being cruel to them, but somehow it had made me feel better." He frowned and shook his head as if that would clear his thinking. "I wish I could be different, but I don't know how. I'm all mixed up." He began to cry quietly and angrily brushed the tears away.

Alex continued to stare at the toilet block although he was aware of how Lee was struggling.

"You know," he remarked casually, "I've noticed that, besides often being very angry, you look sort of sad a lot of the time."

Lee just shrugged his shoulders.

"Actually the look on your face reminds me of how I feel a lot of the time."

Lee turned back to look at Alex in surprise. He was shocked when Alex then bluntly asked, "Is someone bullying you?" Lee did not reply, but huge tears chased each other down his face again. Alex went on very gently, "I think it must be your brother, Gary who is causing the problem."

Lee jumped up and stared at Alex. He stood with his fists clenched, his body taught and trembling. At first Alex thought he was going to be punched again, and wondered if he had got it wrong by being so straight. He studied Lee's face. Lee looked shocked, embarrassed and angry, but then his expression changed to one of relief.

He slumped back onto the bench next to Alex.

"I have no idea how you know about my brother, but it's true. It's getting worse and worse. Sometimes I'm scared to go home." Lee sniffed and wiped his nose on his sleeve. He looked at Alex with panic in his eyes.

Alex was beginning to feel a bit out of his depth. He was not sure what to say and he could do nothing himself to help. He stopped to think and began to hear the humming which told him that the angels were with him. He shut his eyes and tried to sort out what he needed to say.

"I don't really know what to say," he finally started, "but I realise that I made a big mistake for ages. I never told anyone about what was happening to me. I just tried to find different ways to cope with it. I know what happened to me is slightly different to you, but I think you need to talk to an adult who is in a position to help sort out what is going on for you at home."

"Yeah, right!" Lee exclaimed. "I told my mum once and Gary found out and beat me up. So that didn't work."

"Oh dear," said Alex. "What I mean is, maybe you should talk to Mr Adams, because he's someone outside your family who has authority and it's his job to look out for the kids in the school."

"You think I'm going to go to Mr Adams? Forget that for a lark!" Lee stood up again as if to walk off.

Alex could still hear the humming. He had to think quickly.

"It's just that I had to see him today," he confessed.

Lee turned back and looked interested.

"I kept the bullying a secret until one day, I told my brother. He told my mum. She told the headmaster and I got called to his office today. I felt really scared at first because I thought that it would just make everything worse, but when I talked to him, he listened and asked me different questions so he could see how it was from my side. It felt like a huge burden was lifted off my shoulders because I realised that he actually cared. He's going to sort it out, even the problem I have with one of the teachers. So, it's worth it.

If I can do it, so can you, because you're much more confident than me. Anyway, what have you got to lose? You said yourself that it's getting worse and your mum can't help. It's worth a try isn't it? I'll go with you if you want."

Alex was out of breath and agitated by the end of this speech. He so wanted Lee to get some help. Lee was standing there with his mouth open. He sat back down again to think. Alex seemed to genuinely care. Perhaps he was right. Things could not get much worse. Then again, he thought maybe he had some ulterior motive.

"Why are you being nice to me when I have been so nasty? Are you trying to get me in trouble?"

"Look," said Alex, "I've been there, even if it's different. I know how bad you feel inside when you can't see any end to it; when you think it must be your fault; when you feel scared a lot of the time; when you feel angry that it's so unfair." He continued, "What had happened between us is over and done with now. You might get told off by Mr Adams for that, but as far as I'm concerned, it's time to move on and make changes."

Lee chewed his lip in concentration. "Okay, I'll give it a go," he said finally.

Alex let out a huge sigh. He did not want to go back to see the headmaster particularly, but it would be worth it for Lee. He gave Lee a playful shove.

"Let's go and see him now!"

Lee nodded and shoved him back gently. They summoned up their courage, gathered their stuff and went into school together. As they walked along, Alex heard the sound of voices singing and knew that the angels were pleased with what he had done so far.

On the way, they met Mrs Anderson, who stopped them just outside the reception area.

"Oh, there you are Lee. I was just on my way to find you. Mr Adams wants to see you in his office."

She turned around to go back the way she had just come. Lee turned pale and grabbed Alex's arm.

"You had better come with him Alex," she said. "Oh," she thought out loud, "you're not in the same class are you? Never mind, we'll sort that out later. It will be good for Lee to have a friend with him."

The boys looked at each other.

Lee was shown into Mr Adams' office on his own and Alex was asked to sit and wait outside. He was finding it hard to think how this might have a positive outcome. Lee was in with Mr Adams for ages. When he finally emerged, he was shaking. Then he was laughing and crying alternately. He sat next to Alex, who put his arm around him and they were both given a glass of water.

When Lee finally calmed down enough to talk, he told Alex, "Mr Adams told me that Gary's been arrested because he beat up my mum. Mum's in hospital but doing okay." He took a sip of his water. "Knowing that Gary won't be there when I get home is such a relief. It made it much easier to talk about how Gary's been treating me." He gave a short laugh. "Mr Adams was very concerned that I hadn't said anything before. He was really upset when I told him some of the things I had to put up with." Lee paused and drank the rest of his water in one gulp.

"What's going to happen?" asked Alex, realising there would be no one at home for Lee.

"I'll be staying with a foster family until Mum's better. They're going to collect me from the reception area at the end of the school day."

Alex thought it would be awful to suddenly have to go somewhere strange, but that was just his worry. Lee seemed really pleased with the idea.

"I'll be having some time off so I can get sorted and visit my mum, but then I'll be back at school," Lee said.

Mrs Anderson interrupted them, giving them notes to take back to class to explain their lateness.

On the way back to their classes Lee said, "Mr Adams told me off for what I did to you. I told him that I'd already apologised and we'd sorted it out. He made it very clear that he never wanted to hear that I was fighting with or bullying any other children."

They came to where they went separate ways. Lee turned to Alex.

"I really am sorry for the way I've been. Thank you for trying to help me." He stopped and looked down at the floor and asked awkwardly, "When I come back to school, will you still talk to me? Will you be my friend?"

"You're on!" laughed Alex and they went off to their classes, both smiling.

The rest of the day seemed to pass really quickly and, before Alex knew it, it was home time. Scott intercepted Alex at the school gate as he made his way out.

"What's going on with Lee?" he asked.

"I can't really say," said Alex, "except that there were some problems at home, but everything's sorted out now." This seemed to satisfy Scott. Changing the subject, Alex asked him, "Have you spoken to Harvey at all during the day?"

"I haven't seen him, let alone spoken to him," Scott replied.

As they neared home, Alex noticed that some of the flowers in Marguerite and Poppy's gardens had already started to shed their petals. The ones that had fallen were scattered on the immaculate lawns like confetti. Alex felt a huge wave of sadness. He knew this was the start of the countdown to their imminent departure. He really would miss them. He felt so snug and safe nestled between their houses.

Willow was ready and waiting for Alex as he went indoors. She was as excited as ever about seeing him. Alex knelt down, gave her a gentle hug and a kiss on the top of her head and whispered in her ear, "I love you so much."

Willow licked his face and then jumped up to Scott for more strokes and pats. Scott was really pleased and went off whistling to the kitchen.

Chapter 23

Alex decided to try talking to Harvey, so he went up to his room and knocked on the door. Harvey did not look his usual, confident self.

"Would you like to go for a walk with me and Willow up to Greenleah Heights?" he asked.

Harvey was surprised that Alex asked him.

"Why would I want to do that? I can't anyway. I've been grounded, haven't I?" He muttered somewhat belligerently, implying that it was Alex's fault.

Alex ignored the tone.

"I think we need to talk," he ventured. He followed up quickly with, "Well it would be better than being cooped up in your room," as Harvey shot him a rather disbelieving look. "Anyway, I'll ask Mum if she'll make an allowance this once," he said.

Harvey's face cleared a little at the thought of respite and he shrugged. Alex took this as an agreement and rushed off to put his case to his mum.

She was sorting clean laundry in her bedroom when Alex rushed in looking a bit anxious and excited at the same time.

"What's up, my love?" she asked. "You okay?"

"Can Harvey be let off his grounding to come up to Greenleah Heights with me and Willow?" he wanted to know.

She looked even more surprised than Harvey and a bit puzzled.

"I want to sort things out with him. I need him to know that it's all okay now and that it's all forgiven and forgotten," Alex continued in a rush.

She sat down on the edge of the bed and looked at her son. He was really quite something. She was amazed at his attitude and it brought a tear to her eyes. She smiled proudly at him and reached out to hold him lovingly by the tops of his arms.

"You certainly are a strange one," she said shaking her head. "If that's what you want to do after all that's happened, then you have my blessing."

Alex bobbed forward and gave her a loud kiss on the cheek before rushing back to Harvey's room.

"Love you, Alex!" she called out after him.

"Come on Harvey!" he shouted, as he galloped down the stairs to get the dog ready.

"Be a minute!" Harvey shouted back as he jumped off the bed and scrabbled around to find his shoes which he had kicked off earlier.

Alex's mum followed him down into the kitchen.

"Your headmaster 'phoned earlier to say that he'd spoken to Harvey, Jimmy, Tommy and Lee. They all owned up to what they'd done to you. It seems they were very remorseful. He said he was assured there would be no further incidents." She continued, "They've been given sanctions for their behaviour. Mr Adams emphasised that he would not tolerate bullying in his school."

She turned to fill the kettle and then went on. "He also said that he'd spoken to Mrs Bartlett, the art teacher. It seems that she hadn't picked up on your difficulties. He explained that she thought you were choosing to sit at the back so you could mess around. She was sorry you'd been so upset. She's agreed that you'll be allowed to sit at the back, but she expects you to work hard and to let her know if you have any difficulties. He also said that if you can't cope, you could change groups."

Alex knew that he would be able to stay in that set because he loved art and was actually getting quite good. He felt very relieved and positive that everything had been sorted out one way or another. Now he could go back to school with no worries and he could enjoy art again.

The brothers walked in silence, each lost in their own thoughts. When they reached Greenleah Heights, Alex let Willow off the lead and they sat on a bench watching her scamper all around.

Harvey eventually broke the silence. "I'm really sorry for the way I've treated you," he said. "I just really felt jealous of you and then after a while, having a go at you just seemed normal. I didn't think about how it made you feel. You know how weird stuff's been happening to everyone? Well, what happened to me made me understand how you must've felt when we picked on you. It was horrible. I'm so sorry. I'll never do anything like that again. I promise." Harvey drew a shuddering breath.

"It's all in the past and all is forgiven," Alex replied simply. It was that easy.

Alex looked out over the view and felt relaxed in Harvey's company for the first time that he could remember. Alex heard a bit of a sniff from Harvey, although he tried to hide it by clearing his throat. He smiled at him and reached out to give him a gentle punch on the arm. Harvey shoved Alex back.

"Do you think maybe we can be mates?" he asked tentatively.

'Mates' sounded good to Alex. "Oh yes, that would be great," he agreed enthusiastically as a wide grin spread over his face.

Just then, Willow came up and nudged Alex to throw the tennis ball. Alex gave it to Harvey. Backwards and forwards Willow raced, fetching it each time Harvey threw it until she lay exhausted at their feet panting. She had a silly grin on her face too.

It was getting late, so the brothers ambled back down the hill. Harvey wanted to pop into the shop for some chewing gum. Alex stood outside with the dog.

Chapter 24

Colin emerged from the alley. He nodded at Alex by way of a greeting. Alex raised his hand in return. Colin lived around the corner from Alex. He was often in trouble and mixed with the wrong sort, according to Alex's dad. Janet, his sister, worked at the shop with Alex's mum sometimes.

Colin seemed really agitated. He was pacing. He kept looking up and down the road and at his watch. He peered into the shop over the numerous posters stuck on the window. He went back down the alley and disappeared behind the shop. Alex thought he had probably gone for a pee. That is why his mum did not like Scott playing in the alley. It stank.

Two men came down the road from the direction of Greenleah Heights and went into the shop. Willow growled at them.

When he returned, Colin saw the men wandering up and down the aisles. He became even more nervous. Something was wrong. Alex looked into the shop too. Harvey was just paying for his chewing gum and Colin's sister, Janet was chatting to Mr Harker, who owned the shop.

Alex began to hear the humming which he was learning to recognise as a warning that he needed to be aware. In any case, he could sense that Colin was in trouble.

He decided to try to hear Colin's inner voice. He focussed on him. He was now anxiously biting his nails and still checking the time. Once Alex had managed to isolate Colin's inner voice, he could understand why he was worried.

Colin was willing his sister to get out of the shop. He knew that he should never have agreed to be the look out on this job, but they had threatened him. He gave up stealing things when he started his college course and he really wanted to make something of himself. He did not know why they had to come back to the area. It was such a mess. He had only just found out that one of the men had a gun.

He wished his sister would stop nattering and get out of the shop. It was almost closing time. He did not want her caught in the middle of the robbery, but he could not warn her, or they would beat him up. They might even kill him as they had a gun.

This was scary stuff. Alex switched off from Colin's inner voice. He was now willing Harvey to get a move on too.

As Harvey came out through the door, Alex immediately grabbed his arm. He pulled him away from the front of the shop, giving him Willow's lead at the same time.

"You've got to trust me," he said in a low and urgent voice. "Take Willow and run home as if your life depends on it. Call the police to warn them that a robbery is about to take place in the shop. Tell the police that there are two men and that one of them has a gun."

This was serious. He knew Alex was not the type to mess around. He had never seen Alex take charge before, but he did not question it. He took a firm grip on the lead and sped home as if the furies were after him, with Willow tearing along beside him. He knew that he needed to do what Alex had asked as he would never have given him Willow if this was not a genuine emergency.

Janet came out of the shop a couple of minutes later, still laughing at something Mr Harker had said. Colin had ducked back down the alley.

She gave Alex a wave, "Hurry up if you want anything in the shop!" she called. "It's almost closing time!" she added.

Alex waved back and smiled.

"Oh, and tell your mum I'll see her tomorrow!" she shouted over her shoulder as she wandered off down the hill.

That just left Mr Harker and the two men inside the shop.

Alex knew he had to warn Mr Harker. He went into the shop. He greeted Mr Harker. "Could I borrow a pen and paper?" he asked.

Mr Harker looked at him quizzically as this seemed a strange request.

Hastily Alex added, "Just need to write down the list before I forget."

Mr Harker was distracted by the men who were wandering up and down, picking up random items that he was sure they would not buy. He absentmindedly handed a pen to Alex. Alex quickly grabbed a flier which luckily had a plain back. He did not want to draw attention to himself by asking again.

Mr Harker had gone off to replace some unwanted items on the shelves. "Hurry along now lads," he said as he passed them. "I'm closing up in a few minutes."

Alex quickly wrote a message.

THOSE TWO MEN ARE ROBBERS. THEY HAVE A GUN. POLICE HAVE BEEN CALLED. LOCK YOURSELF IN THE STOREROOM.'

He pushed it into Mr Harker's hand. Luckily, he knew that Alex was a sensible boy and had already thought that those men were behaving suspiciously. He had thought they might be shoplifters. He now realised he was in real danger. He scurried to the back of the shop carrying some boxes.

"You need to go over to the till," he called to the men. "I will just be a minute." He went into the storeroom and quietly locked the door.

Seeing that Mr Harker was safely out of the way, Alex walked quickly, but calmly out of the shop. He turned the sign on the door from 'open' to 'closed', to deter anyone else from entering the shop. Colin was nowhere to be seen.

Alex waited anxiously by the side of the shop, out of the men's line of vision. Several minutes later, a big police van with its siren on, screeched to a halt outside the shop. One officer pulled Alex out of the way while the others got into position around the front and back of the shop.

"Mr Harker, the owner of the shop, is in the storeroom at the back." Alex informed him.

"Which man has the gun?" he demanded.

"I don't know," Alex said.

"You are surrounded. Come outside slowly with your hands in the air!" an officer shouted through his megaphone.

The men had disappeared from view. Alex thought that they must be trying to get out of the back. He knew there was no way out as there was a cabinet in front of the window and the storeroom door was now locked. He hoped they would not try to shoot their way in as they might get Mr Harker. It was very tense.

After what seemed an age, the shop door opened slowly and the two men stepped outside with their hands in the air. Next, they were made to lie face down on the ground. They were handcuffed and checked for weapons. One man had a knife and the other had the gun.

After the men had been secured inside the police van, Alex was brought into the shop. Mr Harker was shaking the officers by the hand and thanking them over and over again. When Alex was brought in, he rushed over and enveloped him in a bear hug.

"This boy saved me and my shop!" he told the officers and slapped Alex on the back several times.

Alex was then questioned about how he knew what was happening.

"I overheard some talk in the alley," he said.

They obviously did not think he was involved and Alex did not mention Colin. The policemen finished their paperwork and left. One of them slapped him on the back as he went past.

"That was quick thinking, well done," he said.

As the van disappeared from sight, Mr Harker gave Alex another big hug.

"You saved me from being robbed," he said. "Probably saved my life too!" he exclaimed. "Thank you! Thank you! Thank you!"

Alex ducked out of the way of another bear hug. He had had quite enough of all that hugging and back slapping.

"I'm glad I was able to help," he said and hurried out of the shop.

Mr Harker began to lock up.

Outside the shop, Alex breathed a huge sigh of relief and felt very thankful to the angels. He realised that things could have gone very differently. He wondered what would happen to Colin. He hoped he would manage to stay out of trouble. He had been so concerned for his sister. He was probably a good guy when he was not in the wrong company.

Alex did not realise how tense he had been. He shrugged to ease his shoulders, but he felt a bit shaky all over, so he decided to jog home.

His entire family was waiting at the front garden gate and they began to cheer. It was embarrassing.

"You were so brave," said his mum. "Thank God you are all okay!"

"I'm so proud of you!" said his dad.

Then they almost smothered him in a group hug. His dad patted him on the back in congratulations as they went indoors. He was caught up in the moment and had forgotten how strong he was. His patting was more like thumping. Alex was glad when they all got inside and he was able to get behind the kitchen table. Even Willow barked her praise and jumped all over him.

That evening, at dinner, there was a lot of excited chatter in the Angels' household. Everyone thought it was absolutely amazing how Alex had worked out what was going to happen at the shop. They all felt immensely proud of him.

Alex pointed out that it was teamwork that helped to save the day. Harvey's speed down the hill and the quick telephone call meant that the police arrived in time. They all cheered Harvey and Willow barked, which made them all laugh.

Harvey felt pleased that he had been given some recognition and was very proud of his brave brother. Alex noticed that Scott and Harvey seemed to have put their differences behind them as they were now talking to each other again. This was an added bonus.

When all the excitement died down, Alex felt really drained and decided to have an early night. He said goodnight to everyone, had a quick wash and brushed his teeth before climbing into bed. His whole body ached. It had been another incredible day.

He thought about Lee, happy in a new home; Mr Harker and his wife, safe in the flat above the shop; Colin, trying to make a better life; Harvey and Scott being real brothers to him now and his mum and dad so proud. It was not long before he was asleep.

Chapter 25

Marguerite and Poppy were waiting for him in the beautiful garden and were full of gentle congratulations on the use of his gift. They were very pleased with how much he had progressed and the confidence he now had.

"Thank you for all your help," he said. "It was so good to know that you were watching over me. I wasn't scared at the time, but afterwards I did think it might have gone all wrong, so I'm glad you were around."

Alex had an important question to ask.

"When will you be leaving?"

"Tomorrow, when all the flowers in our gardens have shed their petals," Marguerite said sadly.

Alex could not believe it was going to be that soon. He felt anxious.

"You're sure that I'll be able to visit you here, in the garden, when you've gone?" he asked.

They both nodded in agreement.

"Of course you can," Poppy reassured him. "You have our word."

Alex sighed with relief. Then he thought of something else he wanted to know.

"Who will the new neighbours be once you are gone? Do you get to choose? Will they be friendly and kind? Will we like them?"

Marguerite laughingly held up her hand to stop the flow of questions.

"Everything will be fine. You really do not need to worry," she said. "Your new neighbours will be just the right ones for you and your family. You will enjoy having them living next door."

Alex was relieved that it would not just be left to chance.

He had one last request. "Will you visit my mum and dad at our house, before you go?"

"Of course we will," Poppy answered. "I am pleased you asked us, we were going to suggest it ourselves, because we would like to meet your parents again."

"Thank you," he replied.

He could think of no more questions and he drifted gently out of the garden and into a restful sleep.

Chapter 26

The next morning, as Alex set off for school with his brothers, he looked at the angels' gardens and noticed that nearly all the flowers had shed their petals. It was a reminder that it would not be long now.

He realised that he still felt anxious about using his gift well enough when they were not there to give prompts. He knew they would continue to keep an eye on him and would be there to turn to, but he would really miss them being next door.

Throughout the day, Alex found it very difficult to concentrate during his lessons. He did not want to be at school today. He wanted to be with Marguerite and Poppy. He wanted to make the most of the time remaining before they had to leave.

When the final bell went, Alex rushed home ahead of his brothers. As usual, he was greeted at the front door by Willow. He felt the pressure of time running out. He gave her a quick cuddle, put her collar and lead on and whizzed her around the block.

By the time they got home, Alex saw that there were now only a handful of petals remaining on the once lush flowers in both neighbours' gardens.

Poppy and Marguerite were coming out of their front doors. This amazing time would soon be at an end. He bundled Willow indoors quickly and called out for his parents.

They were both in the kitchen. He rushed in and quickly sorted out food and water for Willow and hung up her collar and lead.

"I have a lovely surprise for you," he said. "You need to come with me, out the front, now."

They were curious and made several jokey attempts at guessing what the surprise might be, but they were not even close to the correct answer. Alex felt a little impatient. There was not much time!

"It's really important. You have to come out now," he urged them, beckoning frantically.

They heard the urgency in Alex's tone, so they followed him to the front door. Alex asked them to close their eyes while he opened it. Marguerite and Poppy were standing together on the drive.

"Open your eyes!" he shouted.

Willow rushed out of the house and jumped up at each of the angels, barking and whining in excitement. They both bent to stroke her.

His parents blinked a few times, staring at Marguerite and Poppy. There seemed to be a bright light shining above them. They recognised them instantly. The 'midwives' looked exactly the same as they did all those years ago. They had not aged one bit. Alex's dad walked towards them with open arms. He was really happy as he hugged each of them in turn.

"I can't tell you how much your care and support meant to us when we were frantic with worry over Alex and the doctors did not seem to know what was going on. Thank you so much. We really appreciated what you did for us and for Alex. We have never forgotten you. You were our angels."

They grinned at him and hugged him back.

"We will never forget that day either. It was so special," Marguerite said.

Alex's mum had tears in her eyes, but she was just as happy and pleased to see them again as her husband. She moved forward shyly and hugged them too.

She was too choked up with emotions to say anything except, "The biggest and most heartfelt thank you to both of you."

"Alex is a real credit to you both. You must be so proud of him," Marguerite said with feeling.

Alex's parents nodded in agreement.

"I am sorry to say that we are leaving tonight. We have been asked to return home," Poppy told them. "We have really enjoyed being here, even if it was only for a short while. It has been lovely to see you all again."

She called Willow to her, picked her up and whispered, "You are doing a splendid job of looking after Alex."

Willow wagged her tail enthusiastically and covered Poppy in 'kisses'.

"Okay, okay," she protested with a laugh as she put her down.

They said their goodbyes and, as Marguerite and Poppy turned to leave, Alex's mum and dad heard the feint sound of voices singing. It sounded divine. Now his dad was sure they were angels.

Alex walked with the angels to the front gate.

"I love you both," he said as he threw his arms around them. "Thank you so much for all your help and support. I feel as if I'm so different now. I know I'll be able to enjoy my life and my gift. You've helped me to get my family back."

They took turns to hug Alex goodbye. He felt very comforted by their hugs, but tears sprinkled his cheeks.

"You are doing well already. We are so pleased," said Marguerite.

Poppy added "You know where to find us, if you need us."

As they each walked towards their own house, they waved. Alex waved back with both his hands, one for each angel. He knew that he would not see them on Earth again, but looked forward to seeing them in the heavenly garden.

When Alex went back indoors, his mum and dad were waiting for him by the door with Willow. They had another group hug. No one said anything.

Alex climbed the stairs with his faithful dog and found both Scott and Harvey on the landing waiting to give him a hug too. They had seen him outside from their bedroom window. They knew how hard it was for him to say goodbye to Marguerite and Poppy.

Alex was starting to feel like he really had the close, kind and loving family he had always wanted. He knew he would be very comfortable being part of it.

He quickly rushed through his homework, sitting on the end of his bed. Then he jumped off and took Willow down for her dinner and to lay the table.

His mum was very subdued and thoughtful. A lot had happened in the last few days and it was really emotional seeing those 'midwives' again. She wished she had the time to get to know them more.

When everyone was seated at the table, she served up chicken, mashed potatoes, carrots and peas. Somehow, to Alex, the potatoes seemed much smoother and creamier.

Everyone seemed lost in their own thoughts. Alex felt there was a calm and somehow positive atmosphere. After dinner, he helped to clear up and gave his mum a hug before she went off to the living room. She hugged him back. He felt really tired after all the goodbyes.

Willow snuggled up close to him when he got into bed and then they both quickly fell asleep. He was too tired to dream.

Chapter 27

A couple of weeks later, while Alex was still at school, there was a knock at the door. When Alex's mum answered, she was surprised to see Mr Harker. He was holding a bag in each hand.

"I would have come sooner, only I have been so busy," he said. "I have some things for Alex as a special 'thank you' for everything he did to save me and the shop from the robbers." He thrust the bags at her.

She took them and murmured, "Thank you, Mr Harker; this is very kind of you. I don't think Alex was expecting any reward. He was just glad he was in the right place at the right time to help."

"He is a really good boy, Mrs Angel," he replied. "I know everyone is really proud of him. Please tell him 'thank you' again from me and the wife."

She nodded.

He walked down the drive, turning outside the gate to wave.

That night, when Alex got ready for bed, he noticed his mum had not given him a change of clothing for the morning. He went downstairs to ask her where his school clothes were.

She reached beside the sofa for the bags Mr Harker had dropped off earlier. She smiled as she handed them over to him.

"These are a special 'thank you' from Mr Harker and his wife," she told him.

Alex peeked inside the bags. There were clothes in plastic wrappers inside. New clothes! At the bottom of one of the bags, Alex felt something hard. When he pulled it out, he saw a shoe. A new shoe! Alex's face lit up when he realised that Mr Harker and his wife had brought him a complete, new school uniform. He was so excited.

"Wow!" he exclaimed "This is the best ever!" He ran up the stairs to his room with Willow following close behind him. He took the clothes out of their wrappers one by one. It was amazing.

He had a new, brilliant white shirt, new, yellow jumper, new, trousers, new, brilliant white matching socks, and a brand-new pair of black shoes. He even had a new sports bag and kit.

He held the new clothes to his face and breathed in their new smell. He was elated. They smelt so lovely, fresh and new.

He decided to try them on. The crisp new fabrics felt lovely against his skin. Everything fitted and was so comfortable. The shoes were shiny-bright and laced up snugly over his instep. He felt completely different in it all.

He went to the bathroom and looked at himself in the long mirror from every angle. He could hardly believe his new appearance. He felt so good. He looked good too. He also felt inches taller.

Back in his room, he undressed again and arranged everything neatly. Then he had a sudden thought - now might be a good time to take on washing and ironing his clothes himself. He could not bear the thought of his lovely new things ending up in the big saucepan!

He could not wait to wear them to school tomorrow. He always felt a new school uniform would be symbolic of a bright, new beginning.

He snuggled beneath the blankets. In the light, which crept into the room under the door, he could just make out the shapes of his brand-new uniform. He hugged himself, then reached out and stroked Willow. He felt contented and at peace.

Alex really believed that Harvey and Scott could be the kind of brothers he had so longed for. Lee would be back soon and he was looking forward to having a school friend for the first time.

The new neighbours were turning out to be as lovely as predicted. On one side, there was a similar family to theirs. There was a friend for his mum and two, football crazy boys for Scott and Harvey. There was a girl, who was a bit of a mad scientist, for Alex. On the other side, there was a recently retired man and his wife who had a small, friendly dog. The man offered to help out in their garden when Alex's dad was busy at work. His wife loved baking and had already dropped off some rock cakes and ginger biscuits for them. And their wonderful dog, who absolutely adored walking and playing with Willow.

Alex's parents said that they were all going to visit Gran at the weekend and that they would try to arrange some sort of family day out every so often.

They wanted to make sure that they had some leisure time together as a family so that they could strengthen bonds and ensure the boys felt so secure that they could talk about any of their problems or feelings. They had come through a rough time, feeling much stronger and united.

As for his 'special gift', Alex felt that he would be able to manage this for good and trusted the angels to guide him still. He accepted and cherished his differences.

Now, he saw himself as 'the angel in the middle' in a new sense.

About the Author

Nicola Hedges spent most of her life in London before moving to the South West with her partner nearly twenty years ago.

She has made some radical changes in career from civil servant to osteopath to teaching assistant. A period of ill health dictated yet another change of direction, resulting in her first work of fiction – *'Cici: A Dog's Tale'*

She continues to explore different ways of writing.

In this period of uncertainty and restriction, writing has given her the freedom to create a separate world of characters and find new ways to express the theme of hope.